SPECIAL PREVIEW INSIDE THIS EDITION
of Ann Burton's upcoming tales of fiery passion, legendary courage, breathtaking adventure, and heartrending betrayal . . .

Jael's Story

Deborah's Story

WOMEN OF THE BIBLE

Rahab's Story

ANN BURTON

A SIGNET BOOK

SIGNET
Published by New American Library, a division of
Penguin Group (USA) Inc., 375 Hudson Street,
New York, New York 10014, USA
Penguin Group (Canada), 90 Eglinton Avenue East, Suite 700, Toronto,
Ontario M4P 2Y3, Canada (a division of Pearson Penguin Canada Inc.)
Penguin Books Ltd., 80 Strand, London WC2R 0RL, England
Penguin Ireland, 25 St. Stephen's Green, Dublin 2,
Ireland (a division of Penguin Books Ltd.)
Penguin Group (Australia), 250 Camberwell Road, Camberwell, Victoria 3124,
Australia (a division of Pearson Australia Group Pty. Ltd.)
Penguin Books India Pvt. Ltd., 11 Community Centre, Panchsheel Park,
New Delhi - 110 017, India
Penguin Group (NZ), cnr Airborne and Rosedale Roads, Albany,
Auckland 1310, New Zealand (a division of Pearson New Zealand Ltd.)
Penguin Books (South Africa) (Pty.) Ltd., 24 Sturdee Avenue,
Rosebank, Johannesburg 2196, South Africa

Penguin Books Ltd., Registered Offices:
80 Strand, London WC2R 0RL, England

First published by Signet, an imprint of New American Library,
a division of Penguin Group (USA) Inc.

Copyright © Penguin Group (USA) Inc., 2005
All rights reserved

 REGISTERED TRADEMARK—MARCA REGISTRADA

ISBN: 0-7394-5912-0

Printed in the United States of America

CHAPTER

1

I first beheld the House of Palms on the same day that I was cast out from my home and family.

That morning my stepmother, Helsbah, returned too early from the market. Later I would learn that my father's shop had been searched by the city guard during the night, and they had ripped the place apart. My rugs and tapestries had been trampled and torn, the best of them stolen. Never had my family been pilfered, not once in the twenty-three years since my father had built his first stall to sell the beautiful weavings from my mother's looms.

Helsbah, who cared only for the amount of coin it would take to repair the damage, left my father to sort through the mess and stalked back to the merchants' quarter. My stepmother's brother served as a minor official at King Khormad's court, and she likely came home to dictate a letter to the house scribe, one that would complain at length about such wanton destruction. Helsbah was an experienced complainer, and doubtless imagined her whining would inspire her brother to wheedle some sort of restitution from the commander of the city guard.

My father's shop had not been the only one to be searched. The day before, the horrifying fate of a caravan, discovered smuggling Semites out of the city, had been made known to all. King Khormad ordered his guards to confiscate the caravan's goods, slit the throats of all the pack animals, and then execute everyone who had traveled with the caravan, Semite or not. The decapitated heads had been placed in gruesome, prominent display around the city markets as a warning to any who might be tempted to sneak others through the great gates.

"No Semite in Riha is safe," my father had said over our evening meal. "The king wants them all in chains, and to be caught aiding or harboring them . . ." He shook his head as if grieved. Unlike other Canaanites born in the city, Robur held no animosity toward the Semites or any other foreign race.

My stepmother, on the other hand, felt no such sympathy. "They are like snakes, the way they slither in our midst. May Baal swallow them all into his fiery gullet."

I bit my tongue, knowing too well I could say nothing. The deep hatred Canaanites felt toward the Semites would never change. I silently resolved to pray as soon as possible for those who had been butchered, and beg Jehovah watch over me and my sister. We were half-Semite, something no one in my family, not even Robur, knew.

So deep was I in my prayers the next morning, I did not hear my stepmother return.

My sister, Tezi, whom I had been quietly teaching our faith, tried to divert Helsbah and warn me by calling out in an overloud voice, "The sun has barely risen. Why have you come home, Little Mother?"

"Little Mother" was what Helsbah insisted we call her, although the only thing small about her were her bead-sized eyes and fly speck of a heart. I went still, hoping she would go into the kitchens and torment the servants.

"Did our father forget something?" Tezi's voice grew even louder, as though she were walking down the hall to my chamber. "But tell me and I shall find it for you."

I heard Helsbah snap, "Out of my way, runt," just before my door slammed open. "Rahab?"

By that moment I had shoved my clay tablets, which my mother had carefully inscribed with all the prayers she knew, under my rug. Before I could rise, however, my stepmother loomed over me. The metallic threads in her costly robe glittered as she turned this way and that, inspecting the small oil lamp, the smoking brazier, and the bulges under the plainly woven mat upon which I had been praying.

"So, Daughter." Helsbah's voice grew as soft as rainwater. "What weave you here? Spells, perhaps?"

"No, Little Mother." I rose to my feet. "Just untangling my thoughts."

I could hardly tell her the truth. My mother, Jezere, had been born Semite, but had concealed her faith from all. Such was the price to be paid, she had told me, for loving a Canaanite. Before my mother had died of lung fever, she had secretly taught me her faith, that of the One God, Jehovah. It was an outlawed religion, especially here in Riha, where Baal and many other bloodthirsty gods were feared and worshipped. Mother warned me to take care and keep my faith concealed, even from my father.

"Robur is a good man, but he fears the king and his Baal priests," Jezere told me a few days before her end, her voice nearly gone from the endless weeks of coughing. "That is why I told him I am Maon, not Semite. Thank the One God that all my family is dead."

"Why did you lie to Father? Why do the king and his priests hate Semites so much?" I asked, confused by the need for secrecy.

"Our God forbids the worship of demons and false gods, as well as sodomy and the sacrifice of children, all of which the Canaanites practice. Such laws were given by Jehovah directly to Moses."

My mother had already told me of Moses, the Egyptian prince turned prophet, who had freed Israel from crushing bondage as slaves to Pharaoh. It was one of the most exciting stories I had ever heard, and I felt privileged to know the blood of such holy men also ran in my veins. "But Mother, the Canaanites do not follow the law of the One God. Why do they care if we do?"

"Beneath their hatred is fear, Rahab. Ours is a true faith, and by killing Semites, the Canaanites think to destroy the righteousness of Jehovah's word." Jezere coughed again, bringing up blood as well as phlegm. The fever had drained the dregs of her strength, yet when I tried to ease her back onto her pallet, she found enough to seize my wrist. "Swear to me now, Daughter. Swear you will teach Tezi, and never reveal your faith to anyone but another Semite."

I loved my mother, and I swore that I would obey her wishes. I had been very careful to do so from that day forth, never speaking of the faith to anyone but Tezi.

Now I would have to lie to keep that vow.

"I was meditating on the hokhmah of Moloch," I told her, although she knew I avoided the temple, her friends from it, and everyone else who worshipped there.

"That was not Moloch's wisdom. You were speaking strange words. Foreign, evil-sounding words." My stepmother was a lazy, greedy woman, but her eyes were not ignorant, and neither were her ears. "Where did you learn this pig's tongue?"

Temper rose inside me, hot and fierce. "It is not—" I clenched my hands and jaw and stared hard at my feet. "It was a simple prayer of praise taught to me by a merchant." It was not a falsehood. I had been giving praise to Jehovah, and while she had spent most of her day at her loom, my mother had occasionally gone to the shop during festival days to help my father sell.

"Lift up the rug," Helsbah said.

I swallowed. My prayer she might not understand,

but the tablets were written plainly in Hebrew. "It is nothing, Little Mother; I beg you not trouble yourself—"

Helsbah's broad hand flashed out and slapped my face. The heavy silver ring she wore collided with my nose, and I felt the warm wetness of blood trickle over my lips.

It was not as if I could not strike back. At seventeen years old, I stood a head taller than Helsbah. I had not half her bulk, but years of lifting and winding heavy skeins and rugs had left my hands and arms strong. I had two years of anger built up inside me, anger at her endless complaints, at her greed for my father's wealth, at her careless treatment of Tezi.

No, I could hit her, and I could hurt her. Had not Helsbah been beating me ever since Father had married her? Such was my anger that I felt sure that with one blow, I could send my stepmother to her knees. That was something I wanted to do, and see, badly. I could wrap my hands around her thick neck, and then . . .

"I could kill you," I said, more out of amazement at myself than any threat. I lifted my hands and stared at them. "It would be so easy."

Tezi appeared at my side. "Rabi, no," she whispered, clutching at my arm, working at my fist with her small fingers. She knew how angry I was; only eight years old, and yet she always sensed so much. "You must not."

I had sworn to uphold my mother's faith, and it commanded me to honor my parents. Helsbah would never be mother to me, but I could not strike the woman my father had chosen as wife. I certainly could not kill her.

As if she knew my thoughts, Helsbah slapped me a second time. "Lift the rug, or are you deaf as well as addled?"

I tasted blood in my mouth, in my heart. *She is not my mother.* "Leave us, Little Sister."

Tezi looked up into my face, and then fled.

Helsbah smiled at me as if she knew and enjoyed my dilemma. "Lift the rug, Rahab, and show me this secret work you do when you should be weaving."

Although it tore at me to do it, I lifted one leg and brought my foot down hard and heavy upon the rug's bulge. Pain speared through my sole, and sundried clay cracked. "Do you mean *this* rug?"

My stepmother's gaze followed the sound, and her fat cheeks reddened. "Show what you hide, now, or I shall call for the rod."

Helsbah was on her third rod. She had broken the first two on my back.

I had never before invited pain upon myself—indeed, I had done much to avoid it—but something inside me had broken. Like her rods.

She was a stupid pig of a woman, and I wasn't going to be afraid of her anymore.

"Oh, Little Mother, please do not *beat* me," I said, my plea delivered in an insolent drawl. At the same time, I casually shifted my weight, grinding the broken pieces under the rug until I felt them crumble.

Distantly I felt grateful that I had not baked them, or I would not have been able to destroy them so easily. "I only wish to *please* you."

Helsbah finally saw that I had no intention of lifting the rug, no matter what she threatened to do, and knocked me aside. She yanked back the edge. My tablets, each carefully inscribed by Jezere's own hand, had been reduced to unreadable gravel.

"You might piece them back together," I said. "Should I fetch the glue?"

She jerked up her head, and lines of hatred formed around her nose and mouth. "You will not dwell another day under my roof."

"It is my father's roof," I informed her, feeling oddly calm, "and you do not decide who lives here." This time she would complain too much, too loudly, and my father would see her for what she was and cast her aside.

"Do I not? We shall see." She tugged me into her arms, pressing my face to her bosom before I could wriggle free, and then shoved me away and walked out of my room.

I should have followed her, but I was too angry. How dare she embrace me like that? I went out to the courtyard, and stood for a few moments letting the rising sun bake off some of my ire before I went to the small chamber where I worked on my mother's looms. There I stayed, working the threads and praying for calm I could not feel.

An hour after Helsbah's return, I heard someone from the courtyard call my name.

Hoping my father had returned, I walked out. My eyes had to adjust from the cool shadowed room to the bright light of the midmorning sun. Thus at first I did not see the people who filled our courtyard. When I could, I saw that most were Helsbah's kin and friends, who seemed equally as attractive as my stepmother. This is to say that they resembled a herd of richly dressed swine.

Helsbah's cronies were not the only ones gathered there. To my surprise, I saw my uncle and his family standing in one corner with Tezi and my father. My uncle lived on the other side of the city, and rarely came to visit.

"Father?" I did not halt until I saw the family scroll in the hands of Jotha, our house scribe.

The family scroll contained the names of all blood kin to Robur, and as such was the most valued document in our home. Kept sealed away in a copper tube, it occupied the place of honor above my father's altar to Anat, the fertility goddess. The scribe rolled it open, something I had only seen once, after Tezi's birth. It was a long scroll, but it was a lengthy list, the names inscribed on it dating back to ancient times. It had been recopied onto new parchment every generation, but the names on the scroll were never changed unless there was a birth, a death, or . . .

"Father?" I looked over at him, but he would not meet my gaze. "What are you doing?"

"Rahab of Riha," the scribe announced, "you were found to be in possession of articles of witchery. You have beaten Helsbah, wife of Robur, and threatened to use such articles to work harm upon her. This renders you unclean and, as such, unworthy of this noble family."

Witchery? Beaten? Unclean? "You're speaking nonsense, Jotha. Are you drunk again?"

"I would see proof," my uncle demanded. He was a wine merchant and had a reputation for being stern but fair.

"Here." My stepmother stepped out and revealed why she had embraced me before. A substantial amount of dried blood—my blood—spattered the front of her robe. She had smeared some of it around her mouth and nostrils as well. As I gaped, she tossed a handful of knuckle bones, carved short sticks, and some strangely fashioned medallions onto the courtyard stones.

Even I recognized the diviner tools of a Chaldean witch. Some Canaanites tolerated their presence, but my father had been cheated by such a diviner and subsequently loathed them all. To find his wife bloodied by one of his daughters, who was also dabbling in Chaldean witchery . . .

Helsbah had chosen her weapons carefully. She must have planned this moment for a long time. "The blood on her robe is mine, Father, but those things are not." He would believe me. He had to.

"Yet I found you casting them, and Tezi heard you threaten my life," Helsbah said, and turned to my little sister. "Did you not, child?"

"But—but—Rahab didn't mean it!" She buried her face in my father's side.

Helsbah gestured, and two burly city guards stepped out of a shadowy alcove. To them, she said, "Take her."

I was as swift as I was strong, but the guards anticipated me, and caught me between them before I had taken ten steps. Their leather gauntlets bruised my skin as they stripped me out of my robes and forced me naked onto my knees.

Outrage and embarrassment nearly made me scream—I had never been naked before the men in my family—but I held my tongue and did not attempt to hide my body with my hands. The guards refused to release my arms, anyway.

Helsbah approached and reached out to caress my head in a strange way.

"I shall sell it," she murmured to me. At first I thought she truly meant my head, until I felt her fingering my hair. The long, straight red hair I had inherited from my mother. "It should fetch an excellent price from the wig maker." She held out her other hand, and one of her cronies placed a shearing knife in her hand.

I felt my throat tighten, but managed, "Father? Whatever Helsbah told you about me, she lied. Believe me, I beg you."

Robur said nothing, did nothing. My stepmother yanked up a handful of my hair and cut it off close to my scalp. I was so shocked that I could not speak.

There before the eyes of my kin, Helsbah sheared me like a sheep. She did it slowly and carefully, dropping each shorn tress into the hands of a waiting servant. I knew that cutting off my hair was a ritual, intended to mark me with the shame I had brought upon my house.

Although I had no words for what was being done to me, I did not make the task a simple one. Throughout it, I twisted in silence, trying to work myself free. The guards' hands grew sweaty trying to keep me in place. Several times they cuffed me hard, thinking pain might coerce me to acquiesce, yet still I fought. Only when my head was bare, and blood ran freely from my nose and mouth, did Helsbah step back.

"You are cast out." She took my hair from her servant and stroked the bright locks the way she would a cat. "I speak not your name, nor do I see or hear you." My stepmother leaned close, as if to kiss me. "If you show yourself here again, I shall see you," she said for my ears alone. "I shall see you dead."

The guards released me. I stood and turned to my father. It took me two tries before I could speak. "You condemn me, your own daughter, on her lies? Father, how could you do this?"

Surely he would give me the chance to defend myself. All I had to do was tell him of Helsbah's lies and that I had been worshipping Jehovah, the way my mother had, and he would forgive me and drive my stepmother from our house.

No Semite in Riha is safe. The king wants them all in chains.

Robur came to me, stumbling over his feet. He

12

finally looked at me, tears running down his lean cheeks, and in his eyes was such pain that I nearly wept myself.

"Why?" he asked, his voice tearing a wound in my heart.

I could not tell him the truth. I could think of no lies to counter those told by my stepmother. I only shook my head.

My father opened his mouth, made a strangled sound, and tossed a servant's frayed, dirty robe at my feet. His last words to me were, "You are cast out." He turned and dragged Tezi, who was crying out my name, into the house.

Somehow I pulled the robe over my nakedness and stood tall. I looked at every face and watched them as they turned away from me. Finally I made to leave, only the echo of my little sister's helpless sobs from the house making me cringe.

"May you die slowly," Helsbah called after me in a pleasant voice, "in the gutters with the other dogs."

"Pray that I do, Little Mother." I did not look back at her. "Pray that I do."

CHAPTER
2

I wandered, knowing not where I walked or caring much of my direction. What did it matter where I ended? I had been publicly shamed, shorn. From this day forth, I was forever outcast among my kin. I would never again be known as Rahab, eldest daughter of Robur the Rug Seller, sister of Tezi, or even Rahab the Weaver. Helsbah and her jealousy and her lies had reduced me to Rahab the Witch, Rahab the Pariah. I reached up and touched the uneven stubble covering my scalp; my hair had been my only real beauty, and she had even taken that from me.

Rahab the Outcast. Rahab the Bald.

I turned corners and walked through archways, uncaring where they led me, deaf to the jeers and laughter of those who spied my shorn head and enjoyed my humiliation. There was a numb logic to my movement. I had nowhere to go. Where I stopped, I would drop. Where I dropped, I would likely die. If

I wanted to end it quickly, all I had to do was find a guard and confess to being a Semite. He would probably take some initiative and behead me on the spot.

No, I could not even give myself that ghastly but swift end. Word of my confession might travel, or people might recognize my face from whatever pike upon which they left my head. Word that might lead the city guard back to my home. While I cared little for a father who had so readily abandoned me, and nothing for Helsbah, I could not let them take Tezi.

I might die out here, alone and reviled, but my silence would buy my little sister's life.

Some unconscious part of me guided my feet toward the southeast corner of the city, to Meshnedef. It was an appropriate destination, this place of lost hope, the one quarter to which my mother had always forbidden me go. In Meshnedef, she had told me, the poorest of the city dwelled in perpetual filth and squalor, ever preyed upon by thieves and madmen. Decent folk never walked its dark and narrow streets, which Mother claimed ran thick with offal and rats, or patronized its shops, which Mother assured me sold only diseased meat and stolen goods.

I became aware of my surroundings only shortly after I had crossed into Meshnedef. It was as if I had stepped over an invisible line that divided the virtuous from the reprehensible, the decent from the licentious. Not that there were written warnings posted, or guards to keep the rabble from intruding on the respectable. Yet the signs were all around me, from the deplorable condition of the unpaved, pitted road to the rotten thatch of the roofs sagging overhead.

The first thing I noticed were the little piles of scat, fresh and old, whole and smeared, that littered the street. Some obviously had been left behind by the four-legged, but others, dropped in nooks and corners, surely had been deposited by those who walked on two.

Raised in a house with an old-fashioned but functional privy, I found the sight repugnant and rather unbelievable. Even in the poorest neighborhoods of my quarter, there were public rest houses for servants and latrine pits for slaves. Were there none here? If not, still, how could one simply relieve oneself so openly, out here in the street?

A pair of skinny stray dogs trotted past me, not bothering to sniff at my hem, intent on a rat slinking out from a pile of rubbish. They cooperated as they went at it, one cornering and driving it out to the other.

Caught as I was between Helsbah and Meshnedef, I could sympathize with the rat.

The chase was silent but brief, and only when its wriggling body lay clenched between the jaws of one dog did the other explode with sharp, indignant barking. The rat catcher swallowed his prize with two jerks of his head and ran off, pursued by his unhappy, unsatisfied companion.

If I was to die in the gutter with those two, I thought,

recalling Helsbah's curse, I would likely have something of a wait.

I tried to dispel my gloom by focusing again on my surroundings. Here nothing appeared to be maintained for even basic sanitary reasons; yet it was not as bad as Mother had led me to believe. Filth did indeed crowd the gutters, but time and rainwater had reduced it to an anonymous sludge. The houses were small, cramped, and poorly thatched, but as I moved into the market, I saw no diseased meats or goods of any kind. The absence of front stalls offering goods on display—perhaps to remove temptation from passing thieves—made the shops seem somewhat tidier than those at our market. Cool shade came from the shops' proximity to the city's towering outer wall, where they were nestled like eggs against a warm feathered breast. The wall itself was wide enough to sport a row of shops high upon its battlements, and formed a barrier against the dry desert wind, which often came off the sands as scorchingly hot as the sun.

The most striking difference was in the dress of the people of Meshnedef. Few people walked the street, and those who did ignored me. I saw no signs of wealth, no fine jewels or collars or medallions of any kind. Indeed, most of the men and women who crossed my path wore no ornaments whatsoever, and dressed in very plain, aged robes, the kind my stepmother would have thought only appropriate for scullery servants or slaves.

As I wondered on exactly what the inhabitants of

Meshnedef spent their coin, I turned a corner and heard the sound of trickling, splashing water. Sweat broke out, prickling over my near-naked scalp, while my throat felt as if I had swallowed a pan filled with hearth sweepings. I had not stopped or rested since leaving my father's house, and my bare feet ached. Perhaps I could beg a drink from the source of the water.

As I followed the sound, I came to the end of the row of shops. There, standing in the deep shadow of the city's great wall was a modest structure, two stories in height. Rather than sharing a wall or two with neighboring buildings, as all of the other shops had, it alone occupied the center of a small, barren patch of land.

I saw no fountain, but someone had planted two palms on the sunny side of the house. The sight of them was almost as cooling as a dipper from a well, and I smiled a little as I watched their wide fronds trail green fingers over trumpet-shaped arcs of plump brown dates that had been protected from the birds by cones of parchment. Small streams of water trickled over them from an odd sort of irrigation spout hanging from the roof of the house over the palms.

I studied the trees. If I could somehow climb the nubbly trunks, I might gather a few dates to go along with my drink. "But do I wish to be a beggar, or a thief?"

A pretty laugh rang out behind me. "Gods, child, such dismal choices. Is there nothing else you can do?"

It was the laugh, not the question, which made me turn around.

Behind me stood a woman in a plain cloak and modest robes. A linen veil concealed her face. The veil also seemed quite simple, but it possessed a finer weave than any I had ever seen. No beggar was she, and when she stepped closer, I backed away.

"No need to be afraid," she said. "I mean you no harm. I am Tiamat." She made an elegant movement with one hand to indicate the house by the palms. "This is my home. It is from me that you consider begging or stealing."

"I shall do neither." I felt her gaze on my bare scalp, and my humiliation stabbed me anew. "Forgive me my words. I was only . . ." Why was I babbling on like this to her? "I shall not trouble you."

Tiamat took a step closer. "I would offer you food and drink," she said. Her eyes were very black in color, and yet gentle, as my mother's had been. "That would not be trouble, now, would it?"

"Yes. No." I would not cry, but the bile coming up in my throat might otherwise disgrace me. "I cannot accept."

"I am zanna, child," Tiamat said. "It is my business to provide for others."

I did not know what zanna meant, or why she would offer hesed to one who so obviously did not deserve any such kindness, but I was tired, and thirsty, and so hungry that the very thought of food made my belly clench.

"I cannot pay you for the meal. All I have is what

19

you see." A filthy robe, a bald head, and empty hands.

"That is fortunate, as I ask for nothing in payment." She was beside me now, and she smelled of some dark, sweetly fragrant wood. "I have not yet had my afternoon meal. If we are to dine together, I should know how to call you."

Who was I now, without a home, without family? "Rahab."

"Rahab." She said it with a certain lilt that made me think Canaanite might not be her native tongue. "It means *one who embraces all*, does it not?"

"Not really. It means *wide, like the river*." I shrugged. "Like my shoulders."

"I see." She began walking and guiding me toward the side door of the house. "You were admiring my date palms. The window of my sleeping room is just there, between them." She pointed. "They whisper to me in the night, in harmony with the mountain winds. They try to tell me their hokhmah nisteret."

I studied the palms again. They stood tall and healthy and fruitful, but they were only palms. "Trees cannot talk. They know no secrets."

"This pair can," Tiamat assured me as she opened the wooden door to the house. "It would be a fine thing to know what they are saying, for they have been here much longer than I. Alas, I cannot speak date palm."

I hesitated just beyond the threshold. "I was driven out of my home today."

Rather than the revulsion I feared, she showed

only concern. "Are you hurt? Have you been beaten? There is a healer—"

"No, I am well." The words I had to say burned in my throat. "My family has cast me out. That is why . . ." I touched my shorn head and dragged in a deep breath. "I would not bring my boset into your home."

"Then you may do as I do with the shame inflicted by others, Rahab," she said, without a trace of disgust or pity. "Leave it outside in the yard."

We entered the kitchen of the house, which contained a very large, stone-encircled cooking pit, tall grain jars, and a ladder rack to which drying bunches of herbs and flowers had been tied. An unfamiliar contraption held a bubbling pot suspended over the coals glowing in the cooking pit. There were baskets of dark green leaves with small yellow flowers; scarlet pomegranates and flat loaves of lehem on a low table by the wall; and a shelf of spice pots and olive oil jars above it. From a strangely colored stone jar, ladles, carved spoons, and whisks sprouted like oddish flowers. Woven mats covered the windows, and thin strips of wood coated with some sort of brown sticky substance hung above our heads. From the few dead insects stuck on them, I realized that they were flycatchers.

I saw many things made of copper, bronze, and silver, which indicated this as a fairly wealthy household. But here, in Meshnedef? How could it be thus? My mother had been so adamant about the poverty and deprivation known in this part of the city.

"My throat is parched, but wine on a hot day and an empty belly make my head ache," Tiamat told me as she brought a jug of sweet water to the table and poured a measure into two hammered-bronze cups. She handed one to me, and I saw the glitter of golden scarab rings on her fingers. "Sit down."

I took a grateful swallow from the cup and lowered myself gingerly into one of the small chairs. It had no arms, so it was more like a stool, and the legs were carved from a black wood to resemble dogs with pointed ears and thin snouts. Bits of shell and bone were hammered into the wood, as well as tiny sparkling stones for the dog's eyes.

Tiamat removed her outer cloak and hung it on a peg before unwinding her linen head veil. The weave of her clothing made me wonder who had made them; the quality was far superior to what could be had at market. Long hair, as jet black as her eyes, fell to her elbows. Tiny beads glittered along the narrow braided cables scattered through her hair. Her features were older, and her skin more golden than I had expected, but that was not what riveted my gaze.

A straight fringe of hair covered Tiamat's brow, and cosmetics tinted her eyelids, cheeks, and lips. Studs with polished stones of lapis twinkled in the long lobes of her ears, and a wide lapis and onyx beaded collar lay around her throat. The color of her skin and the gleaming lines of green-black kohl that rimmed her eyes and extended out onto her temples, however, made her heritage apparent.

"You are Egyptian," I said, bewildered. I knew of her exotic people, a few of whom lived in Riha, but I had never actually seen one up close. Such important foreigners were very wealthy and lived within the citadel walls, where they had ready access to the king and his court.

"I was born here, in Jericho," Tiamat said, using the outsider's name for our city. "My mother came from Luxor." She folded her head veil and set it on a smaller table near the door. "She was nursemaid to the children of the house of Imohatep, near the court of your king." She came to sit beside me.

Just how wealthy and influential was this woman? What in Jehovah's name was she doing living here? "Did your father serve the king?"

"I cannot say, as I never met him." Tiamat's red lips curved as she handed me a round of lehem and a bowl of figs. Her three scarab rings were carved from lapis, jade, and onyx, and had small gold dots in the center of each stone. "Now, eat."

Tiamat ate little herself, but talked a great deal. She spoke of inconsequential things, such as the rising cost of flax, and the poor quality of the wine brought in from the south, thanks to the winter drought. She spoke in a light, wry manner, as if the world around her served as nothing more than a mild amusement.

Knowing it might be a long time before I had food again, I ate as much as I could, but the thought of returning to the streets of Meshnedef made it hard to swallow. Now that there were no eyes but Tia-

23

mat's upon me, I felt as if the strength had been leeched from my bones. Before I grew too ill and tired to stand, I thanked her for the meal and rose.

"It was nothing, I assure you." Her easy smile faded. "Where will you go now?"

"I do not know." I had never gone anywhere without my family or a proper chaperon. "Are there outcasts here in Meshnedef?"

"The miskin live on the street, or in the shadows of the wall," she told me. "I cannot recommend any place the poor and miserable frequent as safe for a young woman."

I looked through the window at the heavy sprigs of dates hanging from her lovely palm trees. "Perhaps that is best."

"There is no chance of you returning to your family? They will not reconsider their decision against you?" Tiamat asked.

"No." I would not crawl back to beg for forgiveness. Not from Helsbah and her snake's tongue, and not from the father who had shut me out of his heart. I looked around, aware that I was no better than the miskin, and yet I had intruded on this kind woman's life. "I must go."

"To beg, or thieve, or die?" Tiamat shook her head. "My mother faced such choices, when she was cast out of the house of Imohatep. It was what brought her here." She, too, looked out at the two palms. "I am the child of her choice."

"I do not understand."

"You are so young." She studied me with her black eyes. "Rahab, do you wish to live?"

"I cannot say." I thought of Tezi and, strangely, of my mother. "I have lost everything dear to me, except . . ." As kind as she had been, I could not tell her I was a Semite. "My faith."

"Faith alone can be a formidable thing. I once worshipped my mother's gods, but I have found over the years that they are cold and silent, indifferent to all suffering. Perhaps they know my nature is not that of a sycophant." She held out her hand. "I would show you the rest of my house before you go."

"Why?"

Tiamat smiled. "Only so that you may know another choice."

I felt suspicious. There were worshippers of Moloch who sacrificed children and virgins to their fire god. Most were taken to one of the six temples around the city, where it was said a tall bronze statue of the calf-headed god stood. Fresh blood was "fed" to the statue through its mouth each day, and poured over its outstretched arms. Such offerings could also be made privately, in the home of a worshipper, with a priest of Moloch attending. There were laws governing who could be offered, and when, but the laws were not here. I was.

Tiamat might claim to be Egyptian, and dress as one, but that meant nothing. She knew I was an outcast, and as such I would never be missed. "Do you mean to kill me?" I found myself asking.

25

She did not take offense or laugh at me. "No, child. Moloch finds no nourishment for his eternal fires beneath my roof."

I took her hand, and followed her out of the kitchen. The interior of Tiamat's house seemed as peculiar as her kitchen. The rooms on the first floor had open doors, so I could see into them with a glance. There were many more furnishings than I had expected to see. Like those in the kitchen, they were very thin, light, and elegant, not at all like the sturdy fixtures of my father's house. There were so many chairs and tables, too—enough to provide comfort for a dozen or more—but no sign of Tiamat's family.

"I entertain here, in these private rooms," she told me. "My guests are provided with the hesed of food and drink, and comfortable conversation before bed, if they wish it."

I frowned. "You are an innkeeper?"

"I suppose I am, of sorts." She took me to a set of square-cut rocks that formed a stairway to the upper levels. "Let us go upstairs."

Seven rooms made up the second level of the house, far more than I had expected to see. There were wooden latch-hook doors at the entrance to each. On the doors someone had hung dried clay tablets, upon which were written names and numbers. "You must have a very large family."

"Five sisters." Tiamat moved to the third door and opened it but did not go inside. "This is the room used for mut'a, the temporary marriage."

I glanced at the empty room. It looked very com-

26

fortable, much like the bedchamber my father and Helsbah shared. "I did not know marriage could be temporary." A shame my father had not, either. He might have contracted such a thing with Helsbah and spared me and Tezi much grief.

"According to law the mut'a can last a week, a day, or an hour. It all depends on what the spouse is willing to pay for the privilege of the hesed of a temporary wife." Tiamat closed the door and moved to the next. "This is the room used for ayin-yada, the watching." She opened the door to a small space in front of another door pocked with small holes. Through the holes I could see another empty bedchamber on the other side of the second door. There were a great many oil lamps, especially around a raised wooden platform that was covered with cushions. The platform was not in a corner or off to one side, as most sleeping places were, but had been situated in the very center of the room.

Uneasiness settled over me. "Why would someone wish to watch . . ." All at once I understood and backed away from the door. "Zonah," I said, trembling with fury and disbelief. "You are a zonah and you did not tell me?"

Tiamat's eyes rounded. "Rahab, never say such a thing."

"Am I mistaken?" My voice rose to a shout. "Are you not zonah? Do you not sell the use of your body?"

"We do many things here at the House of Palms," she admitted without a shred of shame, "but you must never use that word again."

27

"Why? You are a zonah, a harlot." Did she think I was too young to know what that meant? "You are as low as the filth in the gutters."

She slammed the outer door shut and turned on me. "Now, you listen to me, foolish girl. *Zonah* is a Semite word. Anyone who hears it will report you to the city guard. They will not care where you heard it; they will execute you on suspicion of being a Semite traitor." She seized my chin with her hand and lifted it to look into my eyes. Sadness filled her own. "Khensu embrace us. You are one yourself, are you not?"

My sister! If Tiamat exposed me, Tezi's life would be worth nothing. "No. I—I heard it somewhere in the market. I did not know it was a forbidden word."

"Just so, never say it again." Her expression gave away none of what she thought. "Who told you about harlots? Your mother?" I nodded. "Was she a harlot?"

"No!"

Tiamat nodded. "Then she could not know what it is to be one."

"What decent woman would?" I pushed past her, wrenched open the door, and ran out.

CHAPTER

3

I did not look back to see if she was following me.
Angry as I was, I would have used my fists on
her. Why had I not seen what she was? Why had I
gone, so blindly trusting, into her house? Had the
shock of Helsbah's treachery driven the very sense
from my head?

The streets of Meshnedef were almost empty,
thanks to the blazing heat of the rising sun. Sweat
ran down my neck and the center of my back, and
my exposed scalp began to feel too hot. I made my
way along the street closest to the wall, which was
a little cooler thanks to the shadows cast by the two
dense rows of dwellings that lined it. One of them
had woven woolen shades covering the windows,
and from them I could hear the clacking wood and
whispering threads of busy looms.

Feeling more confident now, I went to the side
door, taking care to stand in the shadow of the house,
and knocked. It opened only a gap, and suspicious

eyes peered out at me from under thick, black eyebrows. "No beggars."

"Please, master," I said quickly. "I am a weaver, looking for work."

The gap widened, and the strong smell of unwashed wool and dyes wafted out. The man's eyes narrowed on me. "You talk like a runaway slave. Step into the light."

I should have found something to cover my head. "I am Rahab, daughter of Robur, from the merchants' quarter."

"Is that so?" The man uttered a rude laugh and flung the door open. "Then why would you seek work here?" He reached out to pull me from the shade, and as soon as he saw my head his expression filled with contempt. "You dare disturb me in my home." He gave me a hard shove, and I staggered to keep from falling to the ground. "Trouble me again and I shall beat you until you spit blood."

The door slammed in my face.

I trudged back to the street. The cry of a hawk drew my gaze up, and I saw winged silhouettes gliding against the gilded sky. I envied them their freedom and self-sufficiency. *If only I had wings so that I might fly far away from this place.*

I stumbled over a loose curbstone and would have fallen, if not for two hands that caught me—hands wrapped in soiled rags and grime, which did not completely disguise the running sores beneath. The man was a bundle of rags, from his feet to his head.

"What do you here, girl?" Fetid breath, sour with

old wine, wafted from the man's bandaged head. I saw a flash of stained, broken teeth. "Tell old Purnok."

"Nothing." I freed myself from his repulsive grip and went around him.

Purnok followed me. "Have you any drink?"

"No, I do not." I had to change direction to avoid a pair of ancient, stick-thin beggars who scuttled out, their hands reaching, their voices rasping out demands for alms. Two children, no older than Tezi, peered out of a window I passed. Crude pigments colored their eyes and mouths, and one of them laughed, the sound as harsh as if made by an old crone.

The further I went down the shadowed street, the more attention I drew. The beggars who could walk trailed after me in an ever-growing crowd. The faster I walked, the more ardently they pursued me, some snatching at the back of my robe. They begged me for alms, food, wine, and pity.

All were obviously the wretched miskin of whom Tiamat had warned me, and it horrified me to think of joining their ranks. But if decent masters like the weaver would not hire me . . .

I tried to lose the miskin following me by going between two dwellings and circling behind them, but halfway down the alley a big, burly man in a patched cloak stepped out of a hidden doorway. He had wild eyes and a knife scar that distorted his mouth into a sneer. "Get off my property, whore."

I backed out and collided with the waiting beggars.

A fat woman emptying a privy pot into the gutter across the street met my gaze, scowled with disgust, and waddled back into her hovel.

"I have nothing to give you," I told them, holding out my arms. "Look at me. I am no better than you."

One miskin, with dirty stumps instead of hands and feet, uttered a harsh sound. "You still have your toes and fingers."

"Wait, young friend." Purnok shouldered his way through the disappointed beggars until he reached me. "I have a place," he said, crowding close, trying to gather me to his side. "If you steal a bottle for me, we can share it." He looked down the front of my robe. "Other things, too."

His offer was more repulsive than his person. "I am not a thief or a harlot."

Another miskin heard this and laughed. "Not yet."

The prediction made me flee. I ran down the street, dodging carts, trash piles, and other beggars who displayed themselves on scraps of blankets beside the street gutters. The farther I went, the worse Meshnedef seemed to become. Shadows swelled, and the stink of refuse and waste grew thick. Eyes peered out from cracks in the walls of crumbling dwellings that were as ruined as their scabrous faces. Flies swarmed around me. Crusted, grimy hands reached for me. Voices called, begged, laughed, and cursed.

I ran to the shadow of the wall, thinking that might hide me from the miskin. My feet splashed through something, and I almost fell into a dark-looking puddle of liquid. It was not water, but it was being fed from dark streams running down the stones of the wall. When I looked up, I saw five pikes driven into the upper ledge, and five severed heads impaled upon the pikes. Their dark hair, eyes, and beards damned them as Semites.

I bent over and retched until there was nothing left in my stomach, and then shuffled away. Only the sound of heavy, rapid footsteps behind me made me look back.

Two large men were following me. Both were cloaked and carried daggers in their hands. Terrified, I changed direction, moving out of the shadows of the wall and hurrying down a side street. There I thought I might be safe, until I saw that the only exits were to a privy pit and a butchering yard.

I almost screamed as strong hands grabbed me and hauled me back into a dark, empty niche. One of them clamped over my open mouth, and I saw blue, green, and black scarab rings bunched under my nose.

"Quiet," Tiamat whispered.

A few moments later the two men stalked by, turning their heads to show their scowls.

"Will the slaver buy a bald wench?" one of them asked.

The other nodded. "As long as nothing else has been cut off." He saw the privy pit, grimaced, and turned to the other exit. "She had to go this way."

When they had gone, Tiamat removed her hand from my mouth, and I turned to her. "Why did you do that? Why do you keep helping me?"

"No one else will." She looked all over me. "Where are you hurt?"

In every part of my soul. "I am not." I glanced down and saw the blood on my feet. "It was from the wall."

"They put more heads up there every day." Tiamat reached down and tore a section of the loose fabric from the hem of my robe and handed it to me. "Cover your head and follow me. Go where I go; do what I do."

Tiamat led me out of that nightmarish place, walking in the shadows of the wall and the dwellings, taking a winding, twisting path that kept us hidden from the miskin. Sometimes she would stop, listen, and draw me back into the shadows until someone passed us.

I walked around the puddle of blood this time, and did not look up at the heads of the slain Semites.

Once we had emerged from the darkness of the wall, I saw the House of Palms. There before it, Tiamat stopped and faced me.

"That place"—she pointed behind me—"is not where you should go to die. If that is your wish, I shall give you a blade and show you what veins to cut open, and escort you to a temple that will welcome your sacrifice." She cast a disgusted glance toward the inner city. "The priests of Moloch are always eager to swill young, fresh blood."

Or shove Semite heads onto their pikes, I thought, staring down at the blood on my feet.

Perhaps it was seeing those heads, or knowing that Tiamat had again saved me, or the terrible escape that she offered. Perhaps it was only thinking of Tezi, and how much I wanted to hold her in my arms again. Whatever it was, it caused something tight and cold inside me to break apart.

"I do not want to die." Tears made my cheeks wet. "I want my little sister. I want to go home."

"Not a day has passed since my mother made the journey to the next life that I have not wanted her," Tiamat said. "Your sister yet lives?"

I nodded, wiping my face with one sleeve.

"Then your home is lost to you, but she is not. You may see her again." She linked her hands in front of her as she seemed to decide something. "Rahab, what would you do for your sister?"

"I would die for her," I said flatly. "She is all I have, all I love."

She nodded. "She must feel the same for you. Is that not reason to live? Even if it means becoming a harlot?"

I wanted to strike her for asking me that, for making me think of what my sister's life would be like in years to come. She would have no one to stand between her and Helsbah now. My stepmother might try to repeat her trick and have Tezi cast out of the family. I could not imagine my little sister running the miskin gauntlet of beggars, thieves, and slavers. She was so timid and gentle that she would never survive a place like Meshnedef. She deserved a good life, a decent marriage, and a house filled with happy children. I could not give her that now. I could do nothing for her unless . . .

The images of Tezi, the miskin, and the severed heads on the wall flashed, one after the other, in my mind.

I could become a harlot, like this woman who had welcomed me into her strange house. Or I could return to the streets to become one with the miskin, hunger, and rats, or face an early death.

Or worse, I thought, looking at the blood on my feet, one that did not come soon enough.

It was not a terribly difficult decision.

I looked at the two palms near Tiamat's house. They stood so straight, slender queens with their thick fronds like crowns of malachite. They seemed almost defiant, blooming and healthy as they were, unafraid of the sun or the wind, the heat or the sands of the desert, or anything that touched them. I began to see why Tiamat loved them.

"Yes," I told her. "I shall live for her."

Tiamat took me to a bedchamber on the third floor of her house. It was small, dark, and sparsely furnished compared to the rooms beneath it, but the sleeping mat was made soft with grass-stuffed cushions, and a light breeze came through the tiny window.

"This is where you will sleep, and no one will intrude unless you wish it," she told me. "Those who serve in the House of Palms do so willingly, in the rooms below, and are only asked to contribute a share of their earnings to cover our household expenses. We do not keep slaves, or those who are not right in their minds, or children."

I thought of the two children with the painted faces I had seen, and shuddered. "What must I do now?"

"Rest." She guided me over to the mat. "We will come and wake you for the evening meal."

After Tiamat left, I went to the small window. It was an open square no bigger than my face, but from it I could see most of the east side of Meshnedef. The streets were almost empty, but the sun was overhead, and citizens all over Riha escaped this, the hottest part of the day.

You are standing in a room in a house of harlots, a frosty little voice inside me said. *About to become a harlot yourself.*

Zonah, Jezere had explained to me, were outcast women who had lost all faith and morals. Unlike Semites, most Canaanites considered harlotry a respectable profession for women. Even I knew of the places around the city where zonah gathered, arrayed in their colorful robes and jewelry, showing passing men coy glimpses of their painted faces; yet my mother insisted that such females were the greatest boset, as repulsive as the hazrata, the courtesans of wealthy men, or the qedesh, the holy prostitutes who served in the temples of Baal, Astarte, and Moloch.

A woman's untouched body belongs to her husband,

37

Jezere had told me after she had explained making the shakab, the greatest intimacy shared by men and women, perhaps afraid that I might be tempted into doing the same with some Canaanite boy or temple acolyte. *It is the gift she brings to her marriage, not something she sells to strangers, or offers on the stone altar of an idol.*

My heart hardened, for I knew there would be no husband for me now. Marriages were arranged by one's parents, and my family would never take me back. Even if I could find a man willing to make me his wife, what had I to offer? Whatever dowry my father had intended for me had been forfeit the moment he had thrown me into the street. Nor could I find work, given the weaver's reaction to my state.

While this harlot offers me food, sanctuary, and work. What did that say about me and my decent family?

I turned away from the window and went to the sleeping mat, but I could not rest. My eyelids did not wish to close, and I spent an hour watching a sunbeam inch slowly down the wall while I tried to decide what to do.

Someone knocked on the door to the room. I sat up and called out for the person to enter.

"Greetings." A stern-faced woman a few years older than me brought in a jug of water, a bowl, and a length of faded linen. "I am Banune." Two long, thick dark brown braids hung over her shoulders, and while she was more square than curved, she had eyes the color of good amber. "This is for you to wash before the evening meal." She set her burdens on the little libation table before she inspected me as she might a thief who had slipped into the house. "Do you know how to use cleansing cream, Unwanted One, or must I show you?"

"I can wash myself without your aid," I said, stung by her insinuation as much as her suspicious regard. "And my name is Rahab."

"Your mother had bad eyes, then, for you are no wider than a poppy stem." Banune placed a small round container of perfumed oil next to the basin.

"Are you a harlot?" I asked.

"I am." She did not seem upset to be called one. "Every woman within these walls is—well, not Cook, she is too old, wrinkled, and cross for any man to wish to buy her pleasures—but the rest of us, yes." Her upper lip curled as she inspected my tattered robe. "You cannot wear that. Have you something a little cleaner?"

"I left all I possessed behind." I glared at her.

"Pity you kept that tongue." Her gaze shifted. "Why was your hair shorn off? Did you disgrace your family by playing harlot for some beardless boy lover?"

I thought of Helsbah's smug face. "I was accused of beating my stepmother and practicing witchcraft on her."

"You do not possess very potent spells nor fists, do you?" She didn't wait for me to answer, but added gruffly, "Tiamat wears many wigs; she will find something to cover your head."

I had taken enough from the mistress of this house. "It matters not. I can wear a veil until it grows back."

39

"So you can, but I doubt Tia will permit it." Banune sounded brisk and not at all sympathetic, but I saw something in her eyes that made the tension leave my shoulders. "Cleanse yourself." She left the room as abruptly as she had entered it.

It felt good to wash my face and hands. I paid special attention to my feet as well, scrubbing with a piece of my robe until all the traces of the Semites' blood were gone. The cleansing cream in the little pot was smooth and lightly scented with flowers and fruit essence. I could do nothing about my bald head, but when Banune returned she had an under tunic, outer robe, and head veil for me to wear.

"You look almost pretty without all that dirt on your face, and you smell better, too. Here are some of my old things. They will serve until Tiamat decides how to dress you." She handed me the clothing. "Change and come downstairs. We eat together in the kitchen."

I held the garments in tight hands. "You offer me your garments without knowing who I am, or what I have done. You do not even like me."

"Do not presume to know my feelings, Unwanted One." The skin around Banune's straight nose crinkled. "Do you intend to kill, steal, or cause suffering?"

I shook my head.

"Then you are welcome in our house." She left before I could reply.

I dressed and covered my shorn head with the veil. Banune's clothes were old, a little large, and a bit too short, but many washings had rendered the light wool soft and comfortable. The fabric had been skillfully spun from white and gray fleece, making me wonder again where such marvelous weavings were to be had.

You are not a weaver anymore, the voice of my conscience lashed out. *You would do better to think of yourself as a harlot.*

I pulled the veil forward so that it hid most of my crimson face and went downstairs.

Tiamat, Banune, and four other women were already assembled in the kitchen and talking amongst themselves. They sat on floor cushions around a long, low table that had not been present when I had first arrived. A fifth, elderly woman brought bowls and platters of food from the cooking pit to them. Each woman seated kept talking but glanced at me with curious eyes. I stood in the doorway, not sure of where my place was to be.

"Ladies." Tiamat stood and clapped her hands, and the chattering voices fell silent. "This"—she indicated me—"is Rahab. She is joining our family." To me, she said, "Rahab, you have already met Banune. This is Arwia, Zakiti, Ubalnu, and Karasbaal." She smiled at each before nodding to the ancient woman at the cooking pit. "Our goddess of the hearth and pantry prefers to be called Cook."

"Goddess my buttocks," was Cook's rude response. "I was born to a cook, married a cook, raised three cooks, and will likely die when I keel over and fall in my own stew pot. What else would you call

41

me? Fool?" She eyed me. "Sit down, girl. The food does not grow hotter."

Gingerly I sat down at the only open space at the table, which was at Tiamat's left hand. Banune sat on her right, and nodded to me.

Arwia, a woman of middle years with light brown hair and a remarkably serene countenance, sat to my right, and passed a plate of ripe dates to me. "I picked these myself this morning, from our palms," she said, her voice low and rather shy. "They're like honey."

Being reminded of the temptation I'd felt to steal some of the very same dates made my face flush, and I only took a few before passing the fruit to Tiamat.

"Where was your bet, Rahab?" Zakiti, who sat at Banune's left, asked. She was very plump and had the largest bosom of any woman I'd ever seen.

"In the merchants' quarter." I looked down at the bowl of steaming broth and vegetables that Cook had just placed in front of me. I recognized the pungent scent of garlic, and my mouth watered. "What is this called?"

"Some outlandish Egyptian name," Ubalnu said. She sat at the end of the table, opposite Tiamat, and had a sly look on her narrow, pale face. Her lips were tinted bloodred and gleamed as brightly as the oiled curls of her intricately dressed black hair. "Our mistress has it three times a week or more."

"The green leaves are meloyikah, simmered with onion, herbs, and taliya before they are poured over cooked barley grains," Tiamat said. "Good for the blood and the digestion."

"I'd rather eat bean stew," Ubalnu said. "All these greens make me feel as if I graze at every meal."

Karasbaal, the only one who had not been talking, looked up. Her frizzy hair had been tinted with yellow ochre, and hid most of her long face, but like Ubalnu she too wore her cosmetics thick and bright. "You make a poor cow."

Ubalnu sniffed. "That you would know."

"Ladies." Tiamat cleared her throat. "Let us not drive off Rahab before she has decided whether she wishes to stay."

"Yes," Arwia chimed in. "Give her an hour of peace before the bickering starts anew."

"We never bicker, do we, Karas?" Ubalnu asked, her smile stretching to a mocking width. "We are *family*, and love each other as sisters under the skin."

"The only skin you love is your own," Karasbaal told her, then gave me a glance. She had deep-set hazel eyes, a large nose, and very thin lips. With a single flick of her kohl-darkened lashes she dismissed me and went back to eating.

I had no appetite still, but I forced myself to eat. The other women talked between mouthfuls, speaking of mutual friends and daily chores as if they were a normal group of matrons. If Tiamat had not informed me that this was a house of harlots, I would never have known. She treated the other women as if they were in truth her sisters.

I thought of my proper family, and how Helsbah had insisted from the moment she came into our home that Tezi and I not speak during meals. She did not want noise while she ate, she had told us, because it gave her indigestion. Of course, talking about herself, her important friends, or nagging my father caused her belly no trouble at all.

Helsbah's lies took my family away from me. Someday, if it is in my power, I shall see that she pays. I swear it.

When everyone had eaten their fill of the meloyi-kah stew, Cook passed around a thick wheel of grainy lehem, whitish goat cheese, and a jug of thick, sweet wine, all of which I refused. My nervousness grew, and I rose and offered my help to Cook, who gave me a sharp look before she put me to work grinding emmer on a large quern atop one of her worktables.

"You need not do that, Rahab," Tiamat said as she came to stand beside me. "Cook can manage."

"I needed something to do with my hands." I scooped some loose grains from the table back onto the quern's smooth stone surface. "You said that you teach your ways to those who do not know them." I glanced at her. "My mother explained the shakab, so I know what is done between men and women. But I have never done it."

"I thought as much." She touched my forearm. "I promise you that it is not as terrible or shameful as your mother led you to believe."

"My mother is dead," I said, sliding the stone once

more over the crackling dried grain. "I am an outcast. Nothing can be as terrible or shameful as that."

"No, you are zanna now. In Jericho, that is a worthwhile thing." A bell rang somewhere outside the house, and Tiamat took the quern stone from my hands and set it aside. "Come now. We have preparations to make for our guests."

CHAPTER
4

Tiamat took me to up to the private quarters on the third floor.

"This was originally my mother's room," she told me as she showed me around the large, lovely chamber.

Like the furniture in the kitchen, everything here was made in the Egyptian light, exotic style, with delicate inlaid woods and vivid paint and lacquers. Chests, small tables, and a vanity with a highly polished bronze disk drew the eye. A standing, four-paneled frame covered with decorated hide disguised a privy stool in one corner. A high platform made of dark wood served as Tiamat's bed, with four legs at the corners carved to mimic lion's paws. A thin pillow covered the raised stone headrest at the top of the bed, and a woven coverlet of a dozen different colors had been neatly drawn over the long cushion upon which she slept.

Once I saw Tiamat's loom, however, I was en-

chanted. It was made in the new fashion of two up-
right wooden posts held in place by stout pegs that
had been driven into the floor. The posts were richly
carved, as were the crossbeams. On it hung a wide
swath of soft white flax warp threads interwoven
with scarlet, blue, and green weft threads. A rod at
the top released more warp as needed, while one at
the bottom gathered the finished cloth in a neat roll.
The narrow, thin shuttle rod had been carved in the
shape of a nimble fish, while the baked clay thread
weights had been molded and painted to resemble
oversize beads.

"This is your work?" I wanted to touch the cloth,
but contented myself with picking out the sophisticated pattern of the weave.

"Yes." Tiamat came to look at it with me. "I never
spend enough time at the loom these days, and none
of my sisters care to learn. Do you spin and weave?"

I nodded.

"No wonder you are always seeking something to
do with your hands. I have another loom you may
use, if you like. Smaller than this one, but better for
wool. In the attic are a great many fleeces we have
taken in trade." She flexed her hands. "I prefer working in flax, as wool makes me itch."

"I melt a bit of mutton fat and rub it into my palms
and fingers before I work with the thread. My mother
said it eases the weave and protects the skin." I
looked around. "Where did you find all these marvelous things? We are so far from Egypt here."

Some of the pleasure left her expression. "My

47

mother's former master, Imohatep, sent all these things to her."

"He was very generous." A princess would have been delighted to sleep here. "But I thought you said she had been made to leave his household."

"Lord Imohatep had an older wife, while my mother was young and quite beautiful. When my mother's master made his annual journey to Thebes to report to Pharaoh, his jealous wife falsely accused my mother of laziness and drove her out of the house." Tiamat went over to the vanity, the top of which held many small pots and jars, and removed a chest from beneath it. "When Lord Imohatep returned from Egypt and learned what had happened, he sent men to search for my mother. Because she had become a harlot, she could no longer care for his children. This greatly distressed him, and so he made this house and its contents his apology for the wrongs done to her."

I watched her open the chest and remove several things. "But you did not care for what he did."

"No. My mother suffered much before he made restitution, and she never recovered from it." She looked down at the three rings on her left hand. "She died when I was still a girl."

No wonder she understood how I felt about my mother. "I am sorry for reminding you of your loss."

"Sometimes even the saddest memories can be welcome." Tiamat took out a wig and set it on the vanity.

The wig, a rich chestnut brown, trimmed and

braided in an Egyptian style, had been stretched over
a form carved from wood to resemble a woman's
head. For a moment, the memory of the heads on
the wall burned behind my eyes so strongly that I
thought I might vomit again.

It is only a wig stand. I repeated that silently as I
took several deep breaths, and gradually my nau-
sea faded.

Tiamat had to notice my reaction, but she only
asked me to sit down on the short stool next to the
vanity.

I had seen my reflection a few times, mostly in
bowls of water and the sides of copper cups, but the
image of my baldness in the polished bronze disk
made me cringe. Helsbah's knife had left only uneven stubble on my scalp. The shame of seeing it
made me close my eyes tightly for a moment.

"No," Tiamat said, as if she knew what I was feeling. "You are not as hideous as you think. For
women, hair is like hope. It is never absent forever."
Her mouth twisted. "Unless you wish it to be."

She removed the wig from the stand. It was longer
than the one Tiamat wore, and had a round inner
pad made of loosely woven fibers, to which locks of
wig hair had been sewn by a deft hand. Carefully
she fitted it to my head, straightening and arranging
it around my face until she was pleased. It felt tighter
than I had anticipated and smelled of the same fragrant wood as Tiamat.

"Now, this is a good piece to wear indoors, or
when it is cool, for it is mostly goat hair and plant

fiber. I have lighter ones, made of human hair, for when you must go outside during the day." She turned me toward the bronze disk. "You make a pretty brunette, Rahab."

The darkness of the hair and the foreign style were not as disturbing as seeing my bald scalp, and I relaxed a little, turning my face from side to side. "No one would know it is me."

"My mother's people never go out in public without wearing a wig, men or women," Tiamat told me as she opened a jar and picked up a fine-bristled brush. "Some of the women even shave their heads bare, like their bodies. Close your eyes now."

I obeyed her, and tried not to twitch as she applied a cool, liquid cosmetic to my eyelids. "I have never worn a wig, or paint on my face."

"If you massage warm water with a little almond oil and fir tree resin into your scalp each night, your hair will grow back more quickly. As for cosmetics, they are not merely for decoration. Kohl keeps insects and strong sun from harming your eyes. No, do not open them yet." Her hands skimmed another, wider brush over my cheeks, and I smelled clay, nuts, and fruit juice. "This is ochre to put some color in your cheeks, and pomegranate juice mixed with oil to make your lips glisten. Do not lick them; let the color set. There are other berries that stain just as well, but they are too dark for your skin."

She plied her delicate brushes over my face for a few more minutes, and then draped me with a lightweight cloth that made a tinkling sound when I moved.

"Do you do this to yourself every day?" I asked, almost afraid to know what I looked like now.

"My mother taught me that a woman does not present a naked face to the world, only to her sleeping cushion, and only when it is not to be shared. There." She turned me slightly. "Open your eyes."

The image in the bronze disk was much different than it had been. My eyes no longer looked wide or frightened. New curves and angles appeared on my countenance where before I had not noticed any. Above my arching brows, tiny circles of copper sewn to the edge of the red veil draping my head shimmered. They were the source of the sound.

I did not look like myself or Tiamat. I looked another person entirely. That might make it easier, if I could separate myself from the image I saw, and let her be the one who did what had to be done.

"You should always wear red," Tiamat said. "The color suits your features and the vibrancy of your coloring. A shame it is so expensive, or we might make you a full wardrobe of red gowns. Still, I think I have just the thing to go with your veil."

She brought one of her fitted Egyptian sheath wraps, and a flowing outer robe to drape over my shoulders. Both had been dyed to a brilliant scarlet.

"Do not think your body as boset, Rahab," she said when I hesitated to disrobe in front of her. Without a flinch, she shed her clothing and stood before me naked. "You see? The flesh is a holy thing, a temple that contains our spirit, and should be respected as well as enjoyed."

Slowly I disrobed. My breasts and hips were larger than hers, and then I felt disgusted with myself for making such a comparison. I started to cover myself with my hands, but remembered Tezi and forced myself to stand as she did. To be naked was to be vulnerable to another, but there was nothing but approval in Tiamat's eyes as she inspected me.

"You have a strong, healthy temple, Rahab." She handed me the garments and dressed as I did.

I tried not to feel pleased by the compliment. "Did you sew these yourself?" I had woven all the cloth for my family, but I was not skilled at piece-making and sewing, which had been done by one of our neighbors.

"They were a gift from Kelles, one of my former guests," she said. "Before he went to the next life, he was a tailor of some talent. Unfortunately, he did not judge color as well as he did the cut of a sheath."

I did not tell her that Kelles had been my family's tailor, nor that I had grown up playing with his daughter Clori. I could not imagine the kind, quiet man I had known coming here to hire Tiamat for the night. Indeed, I felt rather indignant, knowing he once had. What of his daughter? What of his wife?

His wife, who was almost as loud and mean-spirited as Helsbah, I recalled. It was why Kelles had been so quiet; he could never get a word in. Small wonder he had sought out the company of other women.

"I am not as dark as most Egyptians," Tiamat was

saying, "and as I have grown older I find that red and other strong colors make my skin appear yellowish. I only wear light shades now."

Tiamat advised me to save the red clothing for the admiration of men, and wear Banune's old garments until I earned enough to buy some everyday robes for myself.

"These guests, do they come here for the shakab, or must we go and find them?" I asked. I would not go into the merchants' quarter for any reason; I did not want my sister to see me playing the harlot.

"Our reputation is such that our guests come to us, often on a regular basis. But you need not concern yourself with that. For now, you will only serve food and drink, assist our sisters, and observe." Tiamat nodded when I gave her a startled look. "You need time to see how we are, Rahab, and when you are ready, you may choose your first man for your maiden's night."

I frowned. "I thought a harlot had to serve any man who offered payment for her."

"Not in my house." Tiamat examined her reflection in the bronze disk and removed her wig. Beneath it, her own hair was cut very close to her head, like a young boy's, and was so black it had a purple gleam. "My sisters and I do not serve men who are diseased in body or mind, or those who take pleasure in blood sports, privy games, or bestiality. When you are ready to serve guests regularly, and a man truly frightens you or threatens to harm you, you have but to call out and one of us will come to your aid."

I thought of the two men who had chased me. "Does that happen often?"

"Sometimes, when a man drinks too much or fails to achieve his tiph'eret during the shakab, he will grow angry. Others simply enjoy hurting women. In time you will recognize men such as these, as well as how best to deal with them." From the chest she took an elaborate curled wig, with long ribbons of hair as black as her own, and placed it on her head. "What do you think? Too full?"

"No, it is lovely." Automatically I reached to straighten some of the curls that had twisted together at the nape of her neck. It amazed me that a woman who could afford such a costly wig would save a homeless outcast like me, much less take me into her household and teach me her trade. "I am grateful to you, Tiamat. I shall do all I can to learn quickly."

She smiled at our reflection in the polished bronze. "Of that, I have no doubt."

My first days serving in the House of Palms passed more quickly than I expected. Almost immediately I stopped thinking of Tiamat and the other women as zonah, and instead thought of them as zanna, the preferred term among Canaanites. With the ever-widening hatred against Semites, I could not be too careful. It was more appropriate as well, for all that my mother had said about the boset of harlots, the reality, like Meshnedef, was quite different.

Tiamat conducted both her household and her trade with dignity and simplicity. Much of her success came from the way she treated those who came each night seeking the services of a harlot. From the moment they arrived, the men were welcomed with warmth, and treated with friendly deference.

The zanna escorted each man into the receiving rooms on the first floor, where they were served with food and drink. I saw how friendly and social the zanna were with the men, as if they were friends or relatives instead of customers. There was always much conversation and laughter on the first floor, so much so that it was often difficult to remember that these men had come here only for the shakab.

"We make them feel as if this were their home," Tiamat explained. "This gives them ease and lightens their mood, yet it also reminds them to conduct themselves appropriately."

Any guest could choose to be served alone, in privacy, or join other men in the largest of the rooms on the first floor as they relaxed. It was during this reception period that the men requested from Tiamat a specific woman, or made their choice from those not presently occupied. Once the choice had been made, the guests went with their women to the second floor.

The real business of the house took place in the rooms of the second floor. There the men satisfied their other desires with the shakab, and made payment for it to the zanna, mostly in silver. Each zanna had her own room, a scale to properly measure payment, and behind a little standing screen, a lavatory table and toilet stool. Most guests stayed only for an hour or so, but there were a few bachelors who would buy a mut'a, which entitled them to stay with their zanna for a longer period, sometimes until dawn.

Tiamat revealed the hidden cache in each room where the zanna put the payment from each man, and kept it there until the last guest left. "If you wish to safeguard a thing from men," she told me as she replaced the privy pot over the cache hole in the floor, and moved the stool to complete the camouflage, "put it in or under something a man would never touch."

During the days, when the house was always empty of guests, Tiamat and the other zanna told me precisely in what manner they served their guests in the rooms on the second floor. At first shock and embarrassment over the details kept me mute and rigid, for I had never heard intimacies discussed as openly and freely as one might household chores. Nor had I imagined such a variety would be involved in performing the shakab. Evidently my mother had described only the very basic form of the act. Yet the women of the house spoke of their work in such a practical fashion that I soon set aside my feelings and concentrated on what I had to learn.

"Discover what manner of the shakab pleases a man most," Tiamat advised me, "and he will become a regular of yours."

Of regular guests we had many, and by watching and comparing them I saw that each zanna seemed

to appeal to a certain type of man. Zakiti often enter-
tained the youngest of our guests, who were as
drawn to her easy, congenial manner as much as they
were to her substantial bosom. Banune was popular
with men of middle years, who appreciated her caus-
tic tongue and no-nonsense demeanor. Arwia often
attracted the oldest men, who seemed to find her
sedate composure as fetching as her calm beauty. The
most sophisticated of the guests sought out Tiamat,
whose wit and assuredness effortlessly matched their
own, while Ubalnu seemed to appeal mainly to those
far more timid and unsure of themselves.

Ubalnu puzzled me, for she was the only zanna
who showed little deference toward our guests. Indeed, the more interest a man showed her, the more
contemptuous she became. Yet men came to the
house each night to see her, and often had to wait
their turn.

"Why do men desire Ubalnu so much?" I asked
Tiamat once. "She treats them with such contempt
and disrespect. It is as if she is the man and they
the women."

"Some find their desires only when forced into a
more passive role," she told me. "Ubalnu's personal-
ity is such that she is naturally aggressive; thus she
is a match for such men."

The only woman who did not welcome guests with
us was Karasbaal, for she was never at the house
when they came. Each night she left before the first
men arrived, presumably to ply her trade elsewhere,

and she rarely returned until the early hours before the dawn. This practice confused me until I discovered her secret.

One afternoon Cook asked me to carry a jug of heated water upstairs for Karasbaal. "I have been up and down those stairs ten times this morning," she complained, lifting the hem of her robe to display her swollen ankles. "If I go again, I shall slip, fall, and break my neck."

I suppressed a smile. "I can take the water, and anything else you like, up to the others."

Cook sniffed. "Take a message to Ubalnu, then: if she does not return my rug beater to me, she can keep it and do the rugs for me."

I carried the jug of water to the third floor, and knocked on Karasbaal's door. I waited for permission to enter—such was the household courtesy Tiamat insisted we show each other when in our private rooms—and went in when she called out to me.

Karasbaal was standing naked by the window, but it did not shock me. The zanna were casual about nudity, and the third floor tended to be very hot during midday. When the older woman turned to face me, however, I nearly spilled the hot water all over the floor.

"You are gawking, Rahab." Karasbaal walked over to take the jug from my nerveless hands.

I wanted to rub my eyes like a child, but settled for blinking several times. The vision of Karasbaal did not change. She was plump and pale-skinned, and possessed the upper body of a female (although her breasts were rather small and underdeveloped.) Yet beneath her waist, she had a man's sex.

At least, part of it. "You are a man?"

"I would have been." Karasbaal poured a little water from the jug into a bowl and mixed some sharp-smelling white powder in it. It was the same Egyptian powder Tiamat used to help remove all the hair from her body. He then lifted his male shaft to reveal a jagged scar where the rest of him should have been. "I was made a eunuch before I reached my manhood."

I hardly knew what to say. To flaunt the cruelty done to him—and with such indifference, before a near-stranger—seemed so callous. But perhaps it was just another oddity of the zanna. *Could a half man be zanna? Who would do such a thing?* "Why were you made this way?"

"My former master wished me to guard his concubines, not use them; thus he had me cut as you see. When his fortunes reversed, he was obliged to sell me and several of his women." He picked up a flat thin scraper, dipped it in the powder and water mixture, and began plying it over his arms to remove hair stubble. "Do not look so appalled, girl. There are many like me in the world. Tiamat bought me and freed me from slavery, so I am more fortunate than most."

The bitterness in his voice made me think otherwise. "But if you are not made as a woman, how can you make the shakab with a man?"

He snorted. "I do not service other men, foolish one.

I sell my talents to women. I am in much demand, for as I am cut I cannot get them with child. They cannot come here, naturally, as it is not respectable. Or perhaps they are afraid they might encounter their husbands."

Trying to sort out what he did, how, and to whom he did it made my head whirl. It also shocked me to know that women would pay to make the shakab with someone who was not their husband. But now I understood better Karasbaal, and the cloud of bitterness that always seemed to hover around her—or him. *What does one call a man who dresses as a woman and yet serves them as well?*

Suddenly I realized what wretchedness Karasbaal had to feel. I was an outcast from my family, but I could make a new life for myself. He would never be a whole man again.

Karasbaal gave me a look of dislike. "Oh, do not pity me, girl. Your ayin-yada time is almost over. When it is, you will be no better than the rest of us."

I hurried out of the room and ran into my own, slamming the door and leaning back against it. The harsh warning had jerked me out of my foolish dream. I earned nothing from serving wine and food and talking of men, nor would I. Tiamat had been very honest about what she expected of me, and how much I would need to contribute to the household.

Karasbaal had likely not intended to give me such a hesed, but what he said had been a kindness of sorts. He was right; I could not go on watching anymore.

I knew what had been holding me back. When I did lie with a man who was not my husband, and make the shakab with him, I would be committing a great wrong against my mother's teachings. *A woman is chaste and keeps herself so until she is married. So says Jehovah.* Jezere had been adamant about this. *Your purity is part of your dowry.*

Now I would be selling it. Yet if I did not, I could not remain here.

Before I took the final, irredeemable step of doing so, I needed to pray and ask Jehovah to understand, and to forgive me this deliberate sin. Yet I had no mat upon which I could kneel, no prayer tablets to read aloud, no incense to burn in my brazier.

Perhaps He will hear my appeal anyway.

I knelt on the bare floor and held between my palms the memory of the tablets that I had ground into dust under my feet. "Holy Protector, it is said that You hear every voice that calls out Your name, and know every heart that believes in You and only You. Perhaps I was meant to live as nothing more than the miskin, but I cannot. Nor can I end my life and leave Tezi alone. I know it is a sin to do what I must do to live here, with these zanna, but there is nothing else, no other way." My prayer seemed so weak and fretful that Jehovah had probably stopped listening to me. I had to offer Him something. Something that had more meaning than my cowardice. "I shall not be a harlot forever. When I have the means, I shall find other work, and a home where my sister may visit me without shame. This I vow on my mother's soul."

I remained in my humbling position for a few more moments before I rose and went down the hall.

CHAPTER

5

When I asked Tiamat to help me prepare for my maiden's night, she did not react with any surprise. She only gave me a long, searching look before drawing me inside her room and seating me before her vanity again.

"Have you been massaging your scalp with the oil I gave you?" she asked as she removed the rather ordinary brown wig she had given me to wear during the days.

"No, I keep forgetting it." It was only partly a lie. I hated touching my bare head, which always reminded me of Helsbah and the boset she had inflicted on me.

"You may not need it, for I already see new growth." Tiamat's palm brushed gently over my head and the new, short hairs covering my scalp. "It will be as it was before, and sooner than you think, Rahab."

Nothing would ever be the same for me. "It matters not." I lifted my chin. "How do I offer myself to the men tonight, and what is the price for making the shakab with a maiden?"

"You must first begin as you mean to go on, and with anger and coldness is not the way." Tiamat tapped my cheek with her finger. "I know what your mother taught you, but if you keep thinking of what we do as immoral, it will eat into your heart. Soon there will be nothing left inside you."

I rather wondered if there was anything left now. "I cannot afford to feel shame, or to have a heart."

Tiamat gathered my hands in hers. Against my hot skin, her golden rings felt cool. "What I do here with you now, is this wrong?"

I looked down. "No, of course not."

"In my heart, there is no difference between holding the hand of a friend and giving pleasure to a man," she said. "With both, you share your warmth and a part of your body. It is a matter of care and affection."

I frowned. "Friendship costs nothing."

"If I am a good friend, you give me your care and affection in return," she insisted. "Is that not a kind of payment?"

The truth of her words made my heart feel a little lighter. "I do not suppose the men will pay to hold my hands."

"No, but some of them will become your friends." The beads woven in her wig made clicking sounds as she shook her head. "We all need something from each other, Rahab. It is within your power to give men ease by making the shakab with them. It is within theirs to pay you for it. Let your work here be a willing exchange, free of boset and regret, and you will always be a respectable zanna."

I released the breath I had been holding in my chest. "I shall try to see it so, Tia."

"That is better." She gave me a fond smile before she went to her chest and lifted off the top. "I have been saving this one for your maiden night." She took out a stand with a wig that had been fashioned to look like a fountain of long, deepest auburn curls.

"For me? But this is made of real hair." Red wigs were so costly that only the wealthiest women could afford them, so I hardly dared touch it.

"It was a dark brown before. I cheated the goddess of beauty and bleached it lighter, and then dyed it with henna and usfur." She took it from the stand and placed it on my head. The pad holding the hair together was so light I hardly felt it, and the curls were so long that they spilled down over my breasts. "Yes, it is as I said. Red brings you to life."

I touched the wig, which felt as soft as my own hair had once been. I would not be able to wear it, had Tiamat's head not been almost the exact same size as my own.

"This was your favorite, was it not?" Her generosity shamed me again.

"You will only have one maiden night. You should look your best. If I were to wear it now, someone would think me ill." She picked up one of her cosmetic brushes and dipped it into a small pot of red lip color. "Now, pretend you are Ubalnu and pout."

When we went down to the first floor, the other zanna were waiting for us. Tiamat did not have to announce that I had chosen tonight as my maiden's night; the other women knew as soon as they saw me in my finery and makeup.

Arwia, always the first to bestow a compliment or a smile, beamed at me. "Rahab, you look as lovely as a winter poppy. All the men will want you."

"Such are the petals of this fine poppy that no one who sees them will pay any attention to me," Zakiti grumbled. "How am I to earn a beqa with her near me? Am I to parade around in my skin?"

"Spare us that vision, I beg you," Banune said. She was always quick to criticize, but after she walked a circle around me she gave me a single nod of approval.

"No doubt the men will fight each other for the chance to be the one who makes the first row in you," Ubalnu said as she stroked a hand over her long, oiled dark locks. "Best hold on to your hair while they do, or it might fly off your head and make their plows wilt."

Karasbaal appeared in the doorway. Now that I knew he was a man, I understood the reason for his thick face paint, elaborate hair styles, and enveloping garments. His vanity was more an effort to disguise his more masculine aspects so that he could better pass as a woman. A man would not be admitted to the house of a woman by himself, while another woman could go in without raising suspicion among the slaves and servants.

"I shall be spending the night in the citadel," I heard Karasbaal say to Tiamat as she went to meet him at the door. He looked over her shoulder at me. "You are sure you do not wish me to make the first shakab with her?" he said, loud enough for me to hear.

"Quite."

That Karasbaal had even thought to do such a thing seemed so insulting as to render me speechless. Did he think I could not choose for myself? In that moment I could well understand why his master had not trusted him around women. Then I met his eyes, and saw something other than bitterness in them. Before I could decide if it was desire or regret, he turned away and left.

I went to stand next to Arwia, who was at the wine table filling goblets for the guests to come. "Does one ever know who another person is, or what they truly want?"

She considered this for a moment. "No, but you learn to make good guesses."

Tiamat came to the table. "Rahab, as I have told you, you are permitted to choose the man with whom you will spend your maiden night. Taking a virgin outside of marriage is so rare that no man who comes here will refuse the opportunity. I only ask that you inform me before you ask the man to make the shakab with you."

This request seemed odd to me. "If it is truly my choice, then why must I tell you first?"

"What Tia hesitates to say is that some men have no skill with innocence," Ubalnu drawled. "She does not wish you to select someone who will make a mess of it. Like Lukur."

"Oh, you do not want someone like Lukur," Zakiti said at once, making a hideous face. "He was always too rough." She patted her ample breasts. "The last time he was with me, the bruises he left did not fade for a week."

"Yet you never refused him, did you?" Banune snapped. To me, she said, "You need not worry. Lukur never comes here anymore. He is too important now."

"Lukur may yet hear of our Rahab, for he has a taste for innocence, and spies everywhere," Ubalnu said. "Maiden blood is said to be so very powerful, too. He may want her to quench Moloch's everlasting thirst."

"That will be enough, Ubalnu," Tiamat said. "He is too wealthy and powerful to come here again, so Rahab need not worry about him."

Her reassurance did not ease the tightness of fear in my chest. I knew of many men with whom I would not wish to be intimate.

"Still eager for your first, Unwanted One?" Ubalnu taunted. "Or do you find you have not the belly for it?"

I ignored her smirking face and turned to Tiamat. "I would be grateful if you would guide my choice."

The men began to arrive a few minutes later. Over the last week I had caught some of them watching me, but when they asked after me they were told that I was not available to anyone. Now those furtive glances became bold gazes and ready smiles as Tiamat discreetly informed them of my new status. No other choice would be made, I saw, until I had made mine, for no man wanted to leave me to the others. Soon a dozen men filled our largest room.

While we served the nightly refreshments and spoke of inconsequential things, I inspected each guest. Most were regular visitors to the House of Palms, so I knew a little of them.

"So tonight you do the choosing, eh, Rahab?" Akhete, who owned an oil press and several orchards outside Riha, was the wealthiest and handsomest of those present, and usually paired off with Tiamat or Zakiti.

"Yes." I admired Akhete's tall, shapely body, which resembled a temple god statue, but he had unpleasantly soft, damp hands and sour breath.

"Do not grow accustomed to that." Darbas, a stout trader of middle years, laughed. He dressed in costly garments, including a copper-banded cap that symbolized his importance in Rihan society. "You harlots cannot afford to be too choosy. Why, if a Semite came here, you would have to take a filthy fleece as payment."

I thought of something Banune had told me of Darbas—that he never removed his cap lest someone

68

mistake him for his brother, a fish seller—and kept my smile easy.

"Now, now, Darbas," said Hlavat. An elderly scribe who had recently retired from King Khormad's court, he was invariably kind and rather protective toward all the zanna. He lived only a few streets away, and always came to spend one night a week with Arwia, his favorite. "Semites are nomads; they would hardly come here."

"Those kelb'lim." Akhete spat on the floor. "They trespass on my lands, steal from my orchards and herds. Do you know when they are caught, they lie and say the thieves are my own men? They breed like vermin, too. No matter how many I have killed, they keep coming."

I looked away from the hatred in his handsome face. Those faithful to Jehovah considered it a sin to tell a falsehood. Likely the Semites he had killed had told the truth and were yet blamed for the graft going on right under his nose.

"No caravan can go unarmed into the north country now because of their raids," Darbas added. "The king should hunt them down before they grow bold enough to attack the cities."

"Hunting them down would leave the cities unprotected," another man pointed out. "Maybe that is what they want. Better to let them cook out in the desert."

"Egypt should send troops to protect us," Akhete insisted. "We have paid them tribute for years; they owe it to us."

The thought of Pharaoh's vast armies occupying Canaan chilled me. The Semites, who my mother told me lived as simply as shepherds, would have no chance against them.

"Egypt is our sovereign," Hlavat reminded him, "and Pharaoh has enough problems with the Sea People. He cannot spare troops to protect our territory, nor should he." He put an arm around Arwia. "Now we are boring these beautiful ladies with our talk of politics."

Darbas chuckled. "Women never understand the trouble we men must go to in order to provide them with their many comforts."

Many comforts? Indignation sizzled inside me. Did Darbas have any idea what life was like for women? How they were utterly dependent upon family or a husband for their keep? What happened to them when that family cast them out? What we then had to do to stay alive?

Tiamat rose and walked by me. As she did, she caught my eye and shook her head slightly.

"Ah, but women provide us with all the true delights in this world," Hlavat said fondly. "Let us not deny them what little they ask of us in return."

The other men present began extolling the many virtues of lovely women, giving me a moment of collect myself. I went to the kitchen to retrieve more fruit for the guest bowls, and on my way out I noticed the one man who hadn't participated in the aggravating discussion. I had never seen him before, so I did not know his name or what he did for a living. All I had seen him do was watch the other men and refuse the wine some of the other zanna had offered him.

As I passed him, I saw his rough, callused hands resting against his strong thighs. I liked men who worked with their hands; they seemed more attractive to me than men with oily, pampered hands like Akhete's.

"You must never argue with the guests," Tiamat murmured as she followed me out of the room.

I glanced at her. "Even when they spout nonsense like that?"

"Especially then. Men never understand what we women must endure to provide them with their delusions." She smiled. "You were looking at Narath. Do you like him?"

"The large, quiet one?" She nodded. "I do not know. Who is he?"

She thought for a moment. "A master builder, staying at a nearby inn, I believe. One of our sisters said he supervises repairs to one of the walls damaged in the last tremor."

Tremors happened frequently in our valley, and while the violent shaking of the ground was usually of short duration, I never liked them. They could be dangerous, as the strongest sometimes caused some older buildings and sections of the city walls to weaken or collapse. "Does he work for the king?"

"I cannot say, but I imagine so. Khormad is certainly a fanatic about keeping the city walls in good repair."

71

Narath was not a particularly young or handsome man, and his body shape was more that of a wide block of stone than a graceful statue. "He has good hands, does he not?"

"Yes. Hands often say much about the man." Tiamat took the bowl of grapes from me. "Would Narath be your choice?"

I was not sure of that yet. "I would like to speak with him before I decide that."

"Very wise." She tucked her arm through mine. "Although it may be a challenge, for I have never been able to coax more than a handful of words out of him. The man is like one of his walls."

On impulse, I picked up a water jug as I left the kitchen, and took it to Narath. Now that I knew he was a builder, I could see other things about him: the way his light brown eyes seemed to measure everything with one glance, the way working in the sunlight had bronzed his skin and gilded his hair, which he wore short-cropped, like a common worker. Like most Rihan men, he kept his face clean-shaven. He was neither handsome nor ugly, but rather ordinary; a man few would give a second glance.

"Do you wish some cool water instead of wine?" I asked, offering the jug.

"Yes." He held out his empty goblet, which I filled, and then took a long drink from it. "I thank you, Zanna."

"I am called Rahab, and I am told you are Narath." I placed the jug aside and sat, as he did, on one of

72

the floor cushions Tiamat had scattered about the room. "You do not like our wine?"

"It puts me to sleep." The side of his mouth turned up. "Not something I wish to do here."

I spoke of my own preference for water or fruit juice, as wine often went to my head, and how sweet the city's spring water had tasted since the winter rains had abated. I did not possess a gift for making conversation, however, and Narath actually said very little in response. He did not seem bored, and in fact paid polite attention to everything I said, but I could tell he was not interested in idle talk.

"The khamsin will be here soon," I said, thinking of the terrible sandstorms that swept over the city during the midst of spring. "Will they hamper the work being done to repair the walls?"

"That work never ceases, no matter what the gods hurl down to plague us." His eyes lit with new interest. "How do you know I am a builder?"

"Men keep few secrets here." I gave him a wry look. "That and I have used up what I can say about the weather. You do not use cosmetics or look as if you weave. Have you lately gone shopping for flax or dye?"

He didn't laugh, but he smiled—a genuine, appreciative smile that warmed me from the inside out. "No, lovely one, I cannot say that I have."

Akhete, who had drunk a great deal by now, staggered over to stand over us. "Come, girl." He held out his hand. "You have kept me waiting while you jabber on to this journeyman. It is time I show you what else you may do with those pretty lips."

Narath rose to his feet, and helped me to mine. "She has not chosen yet, oil merchant," he said, his voice flat, "and I am a master stonecutter and mason, not a journeyman."

"Whatever you are." Akhete made a rude gesture and reached out, trying to latch onto my arm but missing it by several inches. "Why is it so dim in here? Someone light more lamps before I go blind."

"Here, now, Akhete." Tiamat was there in an instant, winding her arm around the drunken man's waist. "You promised to tell me of the sea journey you made over the winter. You are so well traveled, are you not? I have never seen the sea, nor the people who make the purple dye there. Let us find a quieter place where we can be alone." As she spoke, she deftly guided him away.

The other men waiting were not as drunk, and they watched me with the same intensity stray dogs gave anything they could devour. They all wanted to make the shakab with me because I was untouched, as if being my first was some sort of prize. Sickened by it, I turned to Narath. I saw none of that greed in his eyes, only admiration and a curious sympathy, as if he knew how I felt.

I did not know what to say, or do. That was the problem. I was also reluctant to go upstairs so soon after Tiamat—Akhete might see us and cause more unpleasantness.

I needed to be alone with Narath, away from all

eyes, so we could speak freely and without interruption. There were things I would know about him before I made my choice.

"I would go outside for some fresh air," I said at last. "Will you walk with me?"

He nodded and followed me out of the house. Groans erupted from the other men as we left, but I paid no heed to them.

The moon had risen over the rooftops, and shed so much of its luminous light over Riha that it seemed only a murky afternoon. I walked with the master builder to the little oasis garden Tiamat had planted around her palms, where there was a bench made of three heavy stones. The trickling sound of the water from the roof pipe made me think of the day I came to this place.

"That is a good wall," Narath told me, nodding to the section just behind Tiamat's house. "Since it was built, I think it has never fallen."

"I shall sleep better tonight, knowing that." I rested my hand against the segmented bark of one palm. "When I first came here, I thought of stealing some dates from these trees." That had not been so long ago; only a matter of days, really. Why did I feel as if I had been here for years? "I decided not to."

"A wise decision." Narath looked up. "It is a long way to fall. You might have broken your neck." He regarded me. "Have you no kin who can provide for you, then?"

Bitter words rose inside me, as they always did when I thought of my situation; yet I was tired of

ever despairing and blaming my father for his choice
to cast me out. He had acted on the evidence to protect his wife and daughter. Perhaps, in his place, I
might have done the same thing.

"None who wish to." I glanced at him. "Why do
you come here, Narath? Does your wife not please
you?"

"I am not married." His voice changed, became
heavy with regret. "When I can, I buy a little time
with a woman. I would rather have a wife, but it is
not possible now."

"As I would have a husband. Yet all I may ever
have for myself is tonight." I held out my hand. "I
would spend it with you."

He seemed astonished, as if truly not expecting to
be my choice. "Rahab, I am not young, or rich. There
are other men in there, important men who could do
much for you. The trader, or that caravaneer—"

"I do not like any of them." I took a step closer
and laced my fingers through his. "I like you." My
boldness deserted me and I felt my face burn. How
did the other women do this with such ease? "If you
would prefer a woman who knows better how to
please you—Tiamat, perhaps—"

The roughened pads of his fingers pressed against
my mouth, silencing me. At the same time, one of
his big arms went around my waist, cradling me in
a close, light embrace. His warmth and scent enveloped me, and both aroused something in me that I
had never before felt. I was not entirely sure that I
liked the sensation.

"You know what is done?" he asked, his voice gruff now. I nodded. "I am not a small man. I shall be as gentle as I can, but it may hurt."

"So I have been told." I curled one hand around the side of his throat, moving my fingertips through the fine dark hairs on the back of his neck. "But Tiamat did not say it would happen before we join."

His brows arched. "Before?"

"Here." I brought my hand down to my belly. "This thing inside me that aches like a deep bruise."

"That is desire." He splayed his hand over mine and rubbed our palms together in a slow circle, making the ache beneath it spread like warmed oil through my limbs. "It is what men feel when they come here seeking a woman for the night. And you have this for me?" He still seemed slightly incredulous.

In my mind, I heard a wail, as if the ghost of my mother were lamenting my wanton behavior; but she was dead, and I had to live. I made myself deaf to the imagined cry.

"I do." I pressed his hand against my belly briefly before I laced my fingers through his. "Come upstairs with me now, Narath. Share my maiden night with me."

77

CHAPTER
6

Narath stayed with me until dawn. Even as the first glimmer of light appeared at the horizon, he lingered, reluctant to leave.

"My men will be at the site soon, and I must inspect the new supports before they begin laying the stonework." Narath came to stand with me at the window overlooking the garden. His hands rested on my waist. "Have you regrets?"

More than I could ever tell him, but none about him. I turned around. "No, I made the right choice. Did you?"

"The best I have ever made." He caressed my cheek. "I shall see you again soon, lovely one." He draped my bare shoulders with my robe before he left me.

I stood watching until the sun was fully up. My body felt changed and foreign to me now, as if it had been made over by Narath's touch. After what we had done together, I would never see myself—or a man, for that matter—as I had in the past.

How vastly knowledge could change everything.

I went to retrieve the purse Narath had given me for our night together. It was then that I discovered he had left me seven sheqels of silver, far more than we had agreed upon; indeed, more silver than I had ever held in my life. The precious metal felt cold and hard as I closed my fist over one square, notched piece.

Hold it tightly, Rahab, my sullen conscience said. *For this is what you will have instead of a husband, a home, and children. This and making the shakab with men who are strange to you, who will never care for you. Who will, like Narath, only pay you and then leave.*

I carried the silver to my room on the third floor and placed most of it in a storage chest Tiamat had given me. The remainder I wrapped in a bit of cloth and set aside to give to Cook, who managed the household expenses and kept the accounts. Then I removed my wig and garments and bathed before changing into my ordinary robes. I would be able to return the borrowed clothing to Banune, as I had earned enough now to buy my own.

I held the red wig in my hands for a moment, wondering why the sight of it and nothing else was what filled me with disgust. It protected me, covered the boset of my bald head. It even made me beautiful enough to fool Narath into calling me his "lovely one."

I wanted to rip it to pieces, and turned to throw it away from me. That was when I saw the loom.

Someone, probably Tiamat, had placed it in the far corner, along with a large basket of spun wool. I put the wig away and went to look at it. It was a plain loom, hardly more than a child's learning frame, but it was wide and sturdy. The polished condition of the wooden crosspieces spoke of many years of winding and unwinding warp threads. There were notches down each side to help with counting rows and thin copper frame clasps to mark the ending and beginning of a pattern change.

I reached down into the basket and took out a skein of spun wool. It was a blend of white, brown, and gray wool, cleverly twisted and silky as if it were lamb's fleece. From the size of the fibers I knew it had come from a mature animal, but something had been done to it to soften the coarser adult fleece. It slid through my fingers without the slightest resistance, telling me that to weave it would be a challenge and a joy. It would make cloth as light and soft as a warm breeze.

Tiamat had said she would let me use her extra loom, and while I was accustomed to something more sophisticated, this would serve me well. It was not necessary to think while weaving. The rhythm of it was like breathing or sleeping; after a few minutes it became an unconscious thing. Tiamat was a weaver; she knew this.

Was that why she had sent it to me? To keep me from thinking too much?

"Rahab," Banune said. She stood looking in outside my door, which I had left open. "Cook is not feeling well. Come and help me prepare the morning meal."

I put the wool back in the basket and silently followed her down to the kitchen. The door to Cook's room, which lay off the kitchen, remained closed. I started the fire in the cooking pit and bread oven outside while Banune went to milk the goats. By the time I was finished, she returned with a small, brimming pail.

"Pour half in the basin there," she told me as she handed over the milk and went to the pantry for a sack of emmer flour. "Use a little in the dough for our lehem. I shall go and check on Cook." She disappeared into the elderly woman's room.

It seemed rather bizarre to be doing such domestic things when all I wanted to do was return to my room and warp the loom with some of that soft wool. Surely that would keep me from feeling the small aches and tenderness leftover from the long night with Narath. Curious, how I wanted to stretch and laugh at the same time I wished I could flee up to my room and weep at the loom. Was intimacy always so bittersweet, or was it because mine would only ever last as long as the man's money did? Why did the thought of the loom waiting in my room shame me so?

"Her hip pains her too much for her to stand long," Banune said as she came out of Cook's room. "Slice some onions for me, Rahab. I need them for a poultice."

I retrieved a few onions from the vegetable basket and peeled them. I saw the looks she gave me, but I did not want to talk about Narath. "Do you always rise this early?"

"Always. I cannot sleep past dawn or I have a headache for the rest of the day." She came to stand beside me. "The others will be down soon, and they will wish to know how the night was for you. You will tell them."

I stiffened. "It is a private thing."

"No, it is not," Banune said. "Theirs may seem a rude interest, but it is how we look out for each other. What knowledge we can share about making the shakab with a man can help one of our sisters when he goes to her bed."

"You did not ask me about it," I said, slicing the onions with a little more force than was exactly necessary.

"I have already been with Narath." She returned my shocked look without a glimmer of dislike or remorse. "There is no jealousy possible here, Rahab. You made a good choice. I like Narath, and I am happy he pleased you. He is a fine lover."

I wanted to be jealous and offended, but she was right. "I told him that before he left this morning."

"But?"

My shoulders sagged. "It was—I did not know he would—that we would—" I felt terribly embarrassed. "Making the shakab is *nothing* like holding someone's hands in your own."

Banune's fine brown eyes went wide for a moment,

and then her mouth curved. "No, it is not." She began to laugh.

I felt a little indignant, until I saw how funny my words must have sounded, and began laughing myself. When our mirth subsided, Banune and I worked to prepare the meal and discussed what had happened.

"I bled for a full day after my maiden night," she told me. "That scared me more than the act itself."

"I bled only a little, and it stopped after the second time," I admitted.

"Did you use a linen each time?" Banune referred to the small pieces of linen, soaked in honey and acacia, which were kept in a bowl in each room. Tiamat had told me how to push one up inside my body before permitting a man to join with me, so that I would not become pregnant.

"Yes." I felt guilty about that, as well, but I would rather have the guilt than a child without a husband. "What I could not understand was the desire. We hardly slept the night, for the want of touching each other and lying together and just . . . being in each other's eyes. I think I felt it as strongly as he. Does that sound ridiculous?"

"No," Banune said, her voice gentle now. "It sounds the perfect maiden night."

"Perhaps it was." I put the meloyikah shavings to soak in a little warm water and stirred the pot of bubbling barley porridge. "I know I should be sleepy, but I am not."

"You will feel tired later," Banune predicted, "and

you should rest at least two days, to give yourself a chance to heal, and do the same if you ever feel pain after being with a man."

"Being with Narath was worth it." I gazed at her. "It will not be so with other men, will it?"

"Some yes, but most . . ." She shook her head. "It is because men are intent on their own tiph'eret, and each one is a little different in how he does things when he makes the shakab with you." She brought some chopped dates and stirred them into the porridge. "Some men are rough and will not prepare you as Narath did. When you know who these men are, you can make use of a little oil first. Others will wish you to do for them things which you may not like. It is best to learn to do them well, so you may finish them quickly."

I saw how she absently rubbed one hip now and then, and wondered if one of the men she had been with last night was responsible for her pain. "It doesn't bother you, that most men are this way?"

"No. I am paid for the use of my body, not my mind or my heart," Banune said. "It is easier if you find something about each man that pleases you. Narath smells very good, like bread, does he not? And you know he is a considerate lover. Pontilan, one of my regulars, has such soft, curly hair, I can hardly keep my hands from it."

After feeling the lovely wool Tiamat had left in my room, I could well understand that. "What of Darbas?" I could not think of a single thing I liked about him.

84

Banune gave me a droll look. "He makes the sha-kab very quickly, and cannot go more than once a night, thank the gods."

Ubalnu strolled into the kitchen. "You look better today, Cook," she said to Banune before eyeing me. "So, you are maiden no more. How painful was it? I listened for your cries, but we heard nothing. Did he keep his hand over your mouth the entire time?"

I, who never knew how to respond to Ubalnu's barbed words and nasty insinuations, suddenly knew what to say. "Is that what they have to do with you?"

She scowled. "No, for I make *them* cry. You should remember that, Unwanted One." Determined to let that be the last word, she turned to saunter to the table.

"Cook is ill today," Banune told her, spoiling the show of scorn. "If you wish to eat, you must serve yourself."

Ubalnu snatched some fruit from the basket on the table and stalked out.

"Why does she treat me with such malice?" I asked Banune as soon as she was out of earshot. "I have done nothing to her."

"You have done more than you know," Banune said. "Ubalnu must use juniper berry juice to keep her hair so dark, and binding cloths on her breasts to save them from sagging."

"What has that to do with me?"

"You do not have to do those things." She sighed at my blank look. "You are *young*, Rahab, and she

85

is not. She envies you, and that envy causes her to be spiteful."

"Oh." I frowned. "That is a silly reason. She was young once."

"Women like Ubalnu covet youth, for they think their only worth is in how young they appear." She rolled her eyes. "And you're right; it is silly. Come, let's eat."

Banune and I shared our meal in a companionable silence, and gradually the other zanna joined us. As Banune predicted, they all wished to know about my night, and I answered them without taking offense. Most of what I had actually shared with Narath, however, I kept to myself. I could tell them he had been gentle with me while not divulging exactly how or the manner in which I had responded to it.

Zakiti decided I was blessed by Asherah for bleeding the first two times I had made the shakab. "That is a good omen; you will have at least two fine, healthy children," she predicted.

"No, it means she will have two lovers," Arwia said, her eyes turning dreamy. "One who makes her a woman, and another who will make her wife."

I glanced at her. "I think I shall have more than two."

"Lovers are not the same as customers," she admonished. "It does not matter how many times you make the shakab, or with whom you make it. Love is not bound by what we do with our bodies."

"Thank the gods," another voice said. "I can live in hope of a wife and marriage again."

We all looked over as Karasbaal came in. He was

wearing his finest robes, and had painted his face so much that it looked more like a garish mask.

"Behold, the Zanna Queen," Zakiti said, lifting her hand as if shading her eyes from the sun. "We are dazzled, Karas."

"You are jealous, 'Kiti. Cook sick again?" Karasbaal said as he raided the porridge pot.

"Her hip troubles her sorely," Arwia said. "Are you not going to greet Rahab? She is one of us now."

He gave me the same odd look he had treated me to before leaving the house last night. "I wish you joy of your newfound talent. No doubt you will make the most of it. You have the look of a natural harlot."

That was meant to hurt me, I thought, but why I could not fathom. I did not care what he thought of me. "I thank you."

Zakiti grinned suddenly, nudging Arwia and winking at me. "Maybe you should go in and tend to Cook, Karas. She does so appreciate your touch." She paused before adding, "So many of the old ones do."

Karasbaal sniffed, sat down with his porridge as far away from me as he could, and ate in silence.

After the other zanna had finished their meal, I scrubbed out the pots while Banune treated Cook with the poultice she had made. It was then that Tiamat finally came to the kitchen. She asked if I was well, but did not press me for details. She also did not wish anything to eat, and only became animated when Banune informed her of Cook's illness.

"I shall send for the healer," Tiamat said.

"Considering how much she hates him, his presence alone should cure her ills." Banune gave her a sharp look. "I would say we should summon him to see to you."

"No, I have taken care of it. Let me know how she fares. Rahab, you will rest today." Tiamat left the kitchen rather abruptly, before I could thank her for the gift of the loom. This time I saw that she did not move with her usual grace.

I also recognized the shadow of worry in Banune's eyes. "What is it? What is wrong with her?"

"You know those men whom I said can be rough? When he is drunk, Akhete is one of the worst." Banune's lips pressed together tightly before she added, "She never complains, but I have seen the blood on her robes after he has spent the night with her."

I remembered how determined Tiamat had been, talking and guiding him away from me last night, and what Ubalnu had said of Tia's concern for me. *She does not wish you to select someone who will make a mess of it.* "How does he make her bleed?"

"More ways than I care to describe. A man can give a woman as much pain as pleasure, Rahab. Never forget that, not even with one such as Narath." Banune sighed. "Do not blame yourself. I shall go and check on her, and if the healer is needed, we will fetch him."

Cook recovered, as did Tiamat, although several days passed before either was able to rejoin the household. During this time Banune took charge of the daily tasks of meals, cleaning, and marketing, and arranged it so that everyone did their share.

It was on a trip to market with Zakiti that I was able to purchase some new garments, sandals, and a little indigo dye for the wool Tiamat have given me.

"For weaving?" Zakiti's plump face wrinkled up with distaste when I explained my purchase. "Why would you wish to weave? You can buy perfectly good cloth and robes here, at the market."

"But I cannot buy them in the colors I wish, nor with the quality I prefer," I told her. A large lump of dye had only cost half a beqa, and mixed with other things, could be made into blue, purple, and even green dye. The wool merchant had not any madder root or other red dye for sale, but it was a rare and costly color, and had to be imported from other parts of Canaan. "That is why I would rather weave cloth for myself."

"If that is your wish." Zakiti never understood why anyone would work when they could sleep or eat, her two favorite activities. "Do you want to stop at the wig maker's stall? There was a caravan that came from Egypt this past week; they are sure to have some new pieces. You will also need henna to keep your red wig bright; Tia likely used most of hers to dye it."

Tiamat had refused to let me return the red wig or take any payment for it; she would take nothing for the loom, either. Perhaps I could buy her a new wig as a gift; that she could not refuse.

"Yes, I would like that," I told Zakiti.

The wig maker's stall was wedged in one corner of the market where there was a little less dust and more shade. The stall had been fashioned like an open-sided temple, and its low counters sported a small forest of stands carved to resemble blank-faced heads. On the heads were wigs in every style, length, and shade that I had ever seen, and many that were completely new to my eyes.

"Greetings to you both, beautiful ladies." The wig maker was a tall man who wore the elaborate curls and embroidered robe of a Midianite. He bowed to us as if we were noblewomen. "May I show you something to make you even more ravishing to behold than you are now?"

Zakiti giggled. "That will take more than a wig."

"Where are your human hair wigs?" I asked, seeing only wool, goat hair, and fiber pieces on display.

"Those I do not keep out where trifling hands might spoil them," he said, surreptitiously inspecting my own wig closely. "Do you seek something in a lighter shade of brown? It would do wonders for those eyes and that smooth skin of yours."

"I want something long and flowing, in your darkest shade of black human hair," I told him firmly. "Not for me. It is a gift for a friend."

He nodded. "The name of this friend? Perhaps I know her."

"Tiamat of the House of Palms," I told him.

"Ah, the Lady Tia, one of my most loyal customers." He slapped a hand over his heart and looked at the ceiling. "A gift from the goddess of light and happiness. I believe I have what only she could wear." He went back behind a partition and emerged a few moments later carrying a gleaming black wig of incredible length and beauty. "This was brought from Egypt; the hair from the head of a princess."

"I did not think princesses were obliged to sell their hair," I murmured, admiring the wig.

The wig maker looked from side to side before bending over and lowering his voice. "Perhaps it was a punishment from Pharaoh, as some say, for a reckless and beautiful young daughter who was found in the arms of an unsuitable lover."

Zakiti gasped, thrilled by the suggestion. "You do not say!"

The wig maker nodded sadly. "Such things happen. One never knows."

I felt the texture of the hair, which was fine but not quite what I imagined princess quality would be. "A fine tale, Merchant. It would even be better if it were true. How much for the wig?"

A gleam entered his eye. "I could not sell it for less than eight sheqels of silver."

"For that much, I could buy a whole person," I countered.

We started to bargain, and by the time we were finished, the wig maker had four sheqels and two beqa of my silver, and I had the wig.

"Henna," I said, remembering that I needed it to refresh my own wig as I took the wrapped parcel from the merchant. "Have you any henna dye?"

His expression turned sorrowful. "No, lady, not since the new ordinance. By order of the city magistrate, no henna or any form of red dye may be sold at market."

That sounded completely ridiculous, and I said as much.

"Shhhh." The wig maker looked alarmed and came out of his stall to stand between us. "This order came directly from the court of the king. You must not be heard saying such things."

"But why would the king choose to ban something as ordinary as a dye?" I demanded. "It makes no sense."

"Whatever the reason, you cannot have it, Rahab. Come," Zakiti said, and tugged on my arm. "I am tired and thirsty, and the sun is burning my skin. Let us go home before *I* turn red and the king bans *me*."

I bid the wig maker farewell and walked down the row of stalls leading to the market entrance. Now that I knew red dye had been banned, I saw what I had not before—the complete absence of the color. Pots that were usually burnished with a red slip were now black, blue, green, or yellow. It was the same with robes, blankets, and carpets. It was as if red no longer existed.

"Why would the king ban a color?" I asked Zakiti.

"How would I know? The king does not confide in me. Wait." She paused, breathing hard. "Do not take such long strides. I must trot to keep up with you."

As I waited for her to catch her breath, a procession entered the market. Two soldiers wearing gleaming helmets and chest plates of bronze made way, waving their sickle-shaped khopesh to clear people to each side. This waving of swords permitted the passage of a large, horse-drawn chariot, richly ornamented with gold and carnelian. Standing beside the charioteer was a dark-skinned man in a bloodred robe. Two lines of men in richly embroidered priests' robes followed the chariot. Each priest carried a torch and wore a red sash around his waist. They all had ritual brands, shaped like calf horns, and burned into the center of their foreheads, proclaiming their devotion to the god Moloch.

"I think I know where all the red went," I muttered.

One of the soldiers shouted out an order for silence, and only when the very air was still did the man in the bloodred robe speak.

"Merchants of Riha," he said in the pervasive, commanding voice of one accustomed to addressing crowds. "Your king, the Great Khormad, who delights the immortal hearts of the gods, and makes tremble the hearts in every mortal breast, sends me with news. Pharaoh's emissaries have arrived, and the mighty god of Egypt has agreed to wipe out the plague of Semites infesting Canaan."

No one cheered, but no one made any other sound.

"In return for Pharaoh's benevolence, and to pay

proper tribute, our fair and righteous king must empty his coffers. When he told me of this, I assured him that the people of Riha would happily aid him in his time of need." White teeth flashed in his dark face. "As of this hour, all merchants and traders will pay a separate tribute tax to contribute to our city's defense and the welfare of the king—"

"We cannot pay another tax, Lord Lukur!" an anonymous voice shouted from the stalls.

"That is the Lukur Ubalnu spoke of?" I whispered to Zakiti.

Her lips thinned as she nodded. "The very same."

I studied the priest's face. His eyes were small and vicious, and so like Helsbah's that I felt my hands clench into fists, and I turned my head away.

"Soldiers will collect your first payment now," Lukur said. "They will return each week to do the same—"

"No!" A man in a frayed robe, his shoulders hunched but his head high, came out to stand before the procession. "You cannot do this," he told Lukur. "We cannot pay any more. We will starve."

Lukur looked down his long nose at the man, whom I recognized now as a basket seller. "I do not ask for much, merchant. Only your due."

"My due, indeed. I now pay taxes to live in my house, to buy our food, and sell at market. I pay a profit tax when I earn and a penalty tax when I do not earn. I pay so much already that my wife and children go hungry every day." The basket seller's voice rose with each word. "I shall not snatch the last of the food from their mouths to pay anything else!"

"No, of course you shall not." Lukur climbed down out of the chariot and went to the furious basket seller. "You are quite right. Your wife and children should not be made to suffer because you cannot keep them and pay your due."

The old man straightened. "No, they should not."

"Where is your home?" After the seller told him of his house, a modest dwelling only a short distance from the House of Palms, Lukur smiled. "That is very convenient, just around the corner. I shall stop there before I go to the citadel, and take your wife and children to the temple of Moloch."

Gasps of fear and outrage spread through the market, while the basket seller turned completely white. "No." He fell to his knees. "No, I beg you, Lord Lukur, do not take them there."

"It is the best solution, do you not see that? Your family will not go hungry anymore, or be a burden upon you," Lukur assured him. "They will feed the great god Moloch, and this will free you to be a proper bid'lem. We must all become true servants of the fire god, for the better of Riha."

Now I understood why the man looked like death. To feed Moloch, Lukur meant to take the man's family to the temple, and sacrifice them.

CHAPTER
7

I cannot say why I did what I did next. Perhaps it was all the terrible things Helsbah had told me. Perhaps it was sheer foolishness. All I knew at the time was, I could not permit this thing to happen.

I shoved my parcel into Zakiti's arms. "Stay here."

She hissed something after me, but I was already darting behind a pottery maker and his young apprentice.

As I made my way behind the horrified spectators, I saw the merchant collapse onto his face, sobbing at Lukur's feet. At the same time, the priests around the chariot produced small drums and began beating them, drowning out the sound of the man's cries.

They beat drums in the temples, Helsbah had told me and Tezi once. *So that Riha is not shamed before Moloch by the cries of the weak and fearful.*

By the time I reached the street, I was tempted to run. I knew how fast chariots were, and suspected Lukur would be eager to carry out an immediate retribution against the outspoken merchant through his family. I might have but a few minutes to reach the basket seller's house before the high priest did. Yet running might draw the attention of the city guard, who were prone to chase anyone who ran. I kept my head down and hurried, walking as fast as I dared and resisting the urge to look over my shoulder.

At last I reached the right house. The basket seller's wife was an older woman who looked as if she hadn't eaten well in months.

As soon as she came out to greet me, I seized her hands. "Your husband spoke out against a new tax. The priest Lukur is coming here to take you and your children with him to the temple of Moloch."

She went very still. "No. This cannot be."

"There is no time," I said, and urged her into the house. "He will be here any minute. What is your name?"

"Evora."

"Evora, where are your children?"

Moving as if hobbled, she led me back through the house to a small room, where her two frail-looking daughters sat working on the half-finished baskets on their laps. Seeing their dull eyes and thin limbs reminded me of the miskin children I had seen.

"Hello, girls," I said, smiling. "I am one of your neighbors, and I have invited you and your mother to share a meal with me. Would you come with us?"

The girls rose obediently, while Evora clutched at my arm. "Where will we go? My husband—"

I could not let her babble on or frighten the children. "We are going to my house. *Now*. Through the back."

I took the girls' hands in mine and followed their mother through the door that led to a pitiful dirt yard where they were trying to grow a small patch of barley. The powerful sun had withered most of the plants, the leaves of which crackled as we made our way through them.

"Cover your head," I told Evora, and put my arms around the two girls, draping them with the sleeves of my robe. When one of them looked up at me with a puzzled expression, I forced another smile. "What is your name, child?"

"Jiela," she said. "My sister is Radani."

"Those are beautiful names. Mine is Rahab." I could see they were tiring, so I picked up Radani and perched her on my hip while keeping one arm around Jiela. "I have a little sister your age. Her name is Tezi."

When we reached the House of Palms, the merchant's wife came to an abrupt stop. "I cannot take my children into that house," Evora said. "It is a—"

"A place where you can rest," I said before she blurted out the truth. "Safely, until we make other arrangements."

She stared at me. "Why are you helping us? We are nothing to you."

I thought of Tiamat, and how she had led me out of the horrific streets of the miskin. I recalled the terrified faces of the merchants at the market. "Because no one else will."

I took Evora and her children in through the kitchen door, and found Cook sitting at the table crushing garlic. The pungent smell was offset by the delicious scent rising from a stew pot bubbling over the cooking pit.

"Cook, this is my friend Evora, and her daughters, Jiela and Radani." I set the little one down on her feet. "I have asked them to share a meal with us."

"Did you." Cook scowled at the little girls, who drew close to me. "They look as if they could use some feeding."

"We have not had much to eat lately." Evora appeared ready to collapse and weep, but she held onto her composure. "Come, girls, let us wash our hands over there in the basin."

I filled three bowls with stew and brought a fresh loaf of bread to the table. "When they have eaten, send them up to my room to rest. Tell Evora they need to stay there, and to keep the girls away from the windows."

Cook nodded as if this were a completely normal request. "You had better go up now and tell Tia about this."

I tried to explain what had happened at the market as simply as possible to Tiamat.

"The man only spoke out against the tax," I said after relating the details of the incident. "That is all.

It is not a crime to protest something. His wife and children should not be killed for what he said."

"So you decided to defy Lukur and rescue them." Tiamat rose from her bed and pulled on a light robe. "You should have thought about this more carefully, Rahab."

"Do you know how offerings are made to Moloch?" I demanded.

The Rihan god of fire had a voracious appetite for blood—human blood—and demanded daily offerings of it, which were poured over the god's statue. The priests could not bleed themselves so often, and so they took blood from worshippers who volunteered to feed the god. To die during such a bloodletting entitled the victim to vast pleasure in the afterlife, with no fear of being cast into the bowels of Mirii, or so the priests promised. Criminals sentenced to death were often handed over to Moloch's priests so the blood from the beheading could be given to Moloch.

There was something else, something terrible they did to children, but my father would never permit Helsbah to speak of it. Since he would not allow her to take me or Tezi to public bloodlettings or temple festivals, either, she would wait until he had left for market before describing them in vast detail to us. The priests of Moloch especially liked using the blood of infants, which the fire god preferred above all others.

"I know how it is done." Tiamat did not look at me. "How is it that you know?"

My stepmother had watched with pleasure the sacrifice of countless babies, and believed that their innocent blood invoked Moloch's protection of Riha and blessings upon all its citizens. She had even dropped hints now and then about the prosperity my father would enjoy if he became a proper bid'lem of Moloch and dedicated me or Tezi at the temple, but Robur disliked the practice of blood sacrifice and adamantly refused to consider the idea.

"My stepmother worships the fire god," I said. "She has told me how they bind sacrificial victims to the wooden asherim before the statue of Moloch." I saw her swallow, and pressed on. "They light all the braziers in the temple, so that they are blazing high as the priests come forward. They use holy daggers to cut the wrists and throats of women, and catch the blood in bowls, and use it to paint the idol."

"And the children?" she asked. "Do you know what will happen to them?"

I did not, as Helsbah would never say. Still, her coy hints had been enough to make me think that the children sacrificed to Moloch died much more slowly and painfully than the adult victims. "No, but I can imagine."

"I rather doubt that." Tiamat went to the window and looked down at the street. "Were you seen going to the house, or bringing them here?"

"No. I was careful."

"When Lukur does not find them, he will assume they are out shopping or visiting. He will take the basket seller into custody and post two guards at the house to wait for the wife and children." She rested her hands against the edge of the window. "If they do not return by tomorrow morning, he will take the man's blood for Moloch."

"How do you know that?"

"I know Lukur." She turned to face me. "You must tell this to the wife. She must understand the consequences." I nodded. "If she does not wish to return to her home, and save her husband's life, what will you do with them?"

"What will *I* do?"

"You have saved them, Rahab. You took them from the only home they have, took them without clothes, food, or any means to pay their way. They have nothing but you. Thus you are responsible for them now." She made a casual gesture. "Perhaps you thought the woman and her daughters could serve here."

The thought revolted me. "You said you do not keep children or slaves in the house. Jiela and Radani are just little girls. I would not *allow* them to serve here."

The lines around her mouth eased. "What will you do with these souls you have saved, then, Rahab? Hide them in your room? Can you earn enough to keep yourself and three others?"

I knew what she was doing, making me see the consequences of my actions. *She likely asked herself the same questions about me before offering me a place here.* "I shall ask Evora if she or her husband have kin outside Riha who can take her and the girls. Then I shall pay someone to get them out of the city."

Tiamat nodded. "What if there is no kin who will take them?"

"I do not know," I admitted, my voice tight. "But I shall think of something. I had hoped you would advise me. I suppose I was wrong to assume you would."

"You *were* wrong," she said, her face showing the merest glimmer of anger. "You acted on impulse. You brought this woman and her children into my house, without my permission to do so. By fleeing Lukur's decree, they are now fugitive criminals. They cannot stay here, and it is too dangerous for them to remain in Riha. They are no better off than they were before you intruded on their lives. In fact, I would say that their situation is now as bad, if not worse, than if Lukur had taken them."

"Worse? What is worse than being bled to death for a calf-headed god?" I flung out my hands. "Do not tell me that you would have let that fanatic priest kill them, to save yourself some inconvenience?"

"There is something you must learn before you interfere with another person's life," she said, very calmly. "You must have the means to help them."

I knew she was right in saying this, and still I could not agree with her. "I shall find a way."

"Very well. I can help you—this time," she warned. "In return, from this day forth, you will think before you act. Even when it seems there is no time to think."

We went to my room, where Evora and the girls were waiting. I introduced them to Tiamat, whom they regarded with wide eyes. Then I asked Evora about her kin, and for once, Jehovah blessed me with some good fortune.

"My brother has a farm outside Haj-baraq, and does very well for himself," Evora told Tiamat. "He has asked us to visit, but we did not go. We could never afford to make the journey." Her eyes darkened. "My husband is a proud man. He would never send word to my brother about how bad things have been for us. Even when I begged him to, for our daughters' sake."

"There is a caravaneer who owes me a favor," Tiamat told her. "He will take you and your girls to your brother's farm." She glanced at the two children. "You must stay there."

Evora nodded, and her eyes filled with tears. "We cannot repay you, mistress."

"Live a long life, and see that your girls grow up to make good marriages. That will be all the payment I require." Tiamat patted her hand. "I am not feeling well, so I shall leave you with Rahab. Be ready to go by nightfall."

When Tiamat left, Evora touched my arm timidly. "I am grateful for what you are doing for us, but my husband . . . what will happen to him?"

"I do not know." This woman had endured enough terror; I would not tell her what Tia had predicted. "If I can, I shall get word to him that you are safe. Perhaps in time he may join you at the farm." I saw that Radani had curled up and fallen asleep on my mat. "You should rest now. You have a long journey ahead of you."

Evora lay down with her younger daughter, while I went over to Jiela. The little girl was standing by my loom and examining the pattern of my weave.

"It is like what we do with the reeds for our baskets," she said, and gently touched the warp threads. "Only the wool is so much softer."

I saw the marks of hard work on her fingers; scars that should not have been there. "It does not have to be soaked first, either." I should have made her go and lie down with her mother and sister, but there was such curiosity in her eyes. "Would you like me to show you how it is done?"

She gave me a shy smile. "Yes, please."

"You must start by warping the loom, which is done with a very long length of spun wool or woven flax." I showed her where I had knotted the beginning of the warp thread around the crossbeam at the bottom of the loom. "You draw the thread up so"—I traced the first warp thread to the top crossbeam—"loop it over here, and draw it back down again. Pluck the thread with your finger; do you feel the tension? It must be snug, but not so much that you cannot lift the thread."

"Like the string of a lyre?"

"Not quite that tight. You must have some give so that you can weave the warp with the weft." I showed her the crisscrossing loops of the warp, and how they were tied off at the top crossbeam. "I always use at least twenty-eight warp threads. This loom can support twice that much, and if the wool is very fine, another half again."

"Will my father come here soon?" Jiela asked me suddenly. "He would like some of that stew the old woman gave us. He is so tired of plain old barley lehem."

"I do not know when your father will join you." I thought of the basket seller on his hands and knees in the marketplace, begging for the lives of his wife and children. At least Jiela had been spared that. "You will be traveling to your uncle's farm tonight. Here." I picked up a skein of wool and handed it to her. "Take this with you. Your uncle may have a loom, and you can start learning how to weave wool while you are staying with him."

She took it and held it against her chest as she glanced back at her mother and sister, who were asleep. She then regarded me with a different expression. "My father is in trouble, isn't he? We are never going to see him again."

"I cannot say." I knelt down so that I could see into her eyes. "Do you know, I cannot see my little sister anymore, but she is still with me, every day."

"How?"

"I see her here." I touched the place over my heart. "All I have to do is remember a happy time I spent with her, and she is with me again."

"But you miss her still?"

"Yes." Of all my regrets, losing Tezi was the one

that cut the deepest into my soul. "I shall miss her forever."

Jiela nodded as if satisfied. "I thank you for the wool." She pressed her lips to my cheek and then went over to lie down beside Evora and Radani.

Evora and the children left that night with Banune, who knew the quickest route through Meshnedef to the gate where the caravaneer Tiamat had hired was waiting for them. Before they left, Evora gave me the little hand basket she carried.

"It is all I have," she told me. "Please, let my husband know we are safe."

I took the basket to my room and prayed to Jehovah for them, as my mother said our God protected the innocent and righteous, and asked Him to guard their journey. I also beseeched Him to make the basket seller's death a quick and merciful one. It did not make me feel better, but it was all I could do.

Before the men began to arrive, I went to give my gift to Tiamat. We did not talk about Evora or the children, and instead I made her laugh by relating the wig maker's unlikely tale.

"It is so long and fine, I can well imagine it belonging to a princess." She stroked the hair with her sensitive fingers. "I dare not ask how much it cost."

"I have cost you more in the last day, I think."

She uttered a soft laugh. "When Banune told me you had brought children into the house, I though what hair I have left would turn white."

107

I grimaced. "As long as it does not turn red." I told her about the ban on red dyes at market, and the new tribute tax. "This Lukur, he wears red boldly enough. Perhaps it has something to do with him."

"You would do well not to run afoul of Lukur again," Tiamat said as she placed the wig carefully in her chest. "He is much in favor at court at the moment, as King Khormad has made Moloch the patron god of his household. That and the ban were likely Lukur's idea."

"Why? Why red?"

"Lukur has been building a new temple to dedicate to Moloch in the center of the citadel," Tiamat said as she went to sit down on her bed. "It is nearly finished, and it will be the seventh temple—seven is the holy number of Moloch. As red is the god's color, Lukur is likely confiscating the dye for something to do with the dedication."

I had heard of temple priests demanding many things, much of which they did not deserve, but never dyes. "Why doesn't he just buy it, like everyone else?"

"Lukur did not become the wealthiest holy man in Riha by paying for things," she told me. "He is too important to come here anymore, but the first time he did, he tried to insist he had divine right to take any woman in the house as his qedesh."

Temple harlots were made to live at the temples within the city, one of the zanna had told me, and made to serve whomever the priests desired them to serve. "Does he have such a right?"

She shook her head. "Qedesh must be sent to the temple as virgins; harlots who make the shakab with common people are considered unclean and unfit under the law. After Lukur's first visit, I had the law copied and put on scrolls, which are kept in every room. In the event he ever comes here and the law slips his mind again." She looked tired. "I fear I shall not be joining you and our sisters tonight."

"Banune wouldn't permit it even if you wished to." I went to sit beside her. Guilt made me say, "Banune told me how you suffered Akhete for my sake. Why did you not refuse him if he is so abusive?"

Tiamat's mouth curled at the corner. "When Akhete is drunk, he is not gentle, but he never causes lasting harm. He is spiteful, however, and if I turned him away, he would use his wealth and influence to do far greater damage to us."

What a decision to have to make. I shuddered at the thought of being obliged to lay with such a man, but that, too, was part of my new profession. "I thank you for what you did for me, but I wish I had known."

"You had a joyous maiden's night; that is what mattered to me. What Akhete did is almost healed." She inspected me. "You are serving tonight?"

"Yes. Banune also spoke to me about what to expect." I could not lie and say I was looking forward to making myself available to any man who desired me. "I am grateful for my time with Narath, and I hope we can be together again. I also understand other men will not be the same when we make the shakab."

"Understanding and doing, as you doubtless discovered, are two very different things. But I have something that may help you feel more at ease." Tiamat removed the green scarab ring from her finger and held it up. "The scarab is a sacred symbol in Egypt. My favorite is the green; that is the color of life among my mother's people." She slid the ring onto my finger.

"I cannot accept this; it is mostly gold," I said, touching it with reverent fingertips. "You have given me too much already."

"I could say the same, but this is not a gift. Or perhaps we will call it the last of my gifts to you. Bring me that cup of water I left on the vanity table." When I fetched it for her, she held it under my hand. "You are to use this only if you fear for your very life, do you understand? Not for any other reason."

"Use what?"

"This." Tiamat turned the carved green stone in the ring on my hand, which revealed a small cavity filled with a scant amount of dark powder. She tapped it, causing the powder to fall into the water and dissolve, darkening it. "I do this with water only so you may see how it works. You must mix it in wine, where the color will not be noticed."

I was fascinated and appalled. "What is it?"

"It has no name. It makes even the strongest man go to sleep within a few moments." She held the cup of water up to my nose. "What do you smell?"

110

"Nothing."

"Exactly. It is said not to have much taste, either."
She set the water aside and held up her hand. "The
powder behind the blue stone takes away most pain.
The powder in the black is poison; it kills."

"Why did you not use the green or the black on
Akhete when he hurt you the other night?" I asked.

"I could not kill him, Rahab, and even the sleeping
powder can be dangerous to use. Some men who
drink it only sleep for an hour; others cannot be
roused for days." She turned the stone of the ring
back into place. "That is why you must use the sleeping powder in your ring only if your life is in danger.
Do you understand me?"

I nodded.

"Wear this ring and you will never feel helpless
against a man." She lay down on her bed and pillowed her head with her arm. "I think we will
both . . . sleep better tonight. I thank you again . . .
for the gift . . . of the wig . . . so fine . . ."

She was asleep.

I pulled the blanket up over her and left her to
go to Banune's room. She was already dressed and
combing out her braids. "Tiamat is feeling a little
better."

"That is good."

I spied the green scarab ring on her left hand.
"Does every zanna in the house have the ability to
drug and kill the men who come here?"

Banune grimaced and went to close the door before
she answered me. "No. Tia is the only one with poi-

son and the pain medicine. She does give sleeping powder to those she trusts."

"You, me, Arwia?"

"Not Arwia, but Karasbaal has one. We watch over the others who do not." She ran a finger over the scarab. "It can be a great comfort, Rahab."

"So can knowing that there are degrees of trust here, and not all are permitted to know Tiamat's secrets." I felt oddly angry.

"I did not receive my ring until I had been here for two seasons," Banune snapped. "Be flattered she trusts you so immediately."

I thought of the strange look that she had given me when I told her of the market incident. "Is it trust, or fear?"

"Am I Tia that I can say why she does something? No." She made a frustrated sound. "Stop worrying about such things and go prepare yourself. With Tia still ill and Arwia gone to visit her family, you will be popular this night."

CHAPTER

8

I was in much demand that night, and the many which followed. Within a moon my knowledge of men, their desires, and making the shakab increased tenfold, as did my determination not to be a harlot forever.

We did not know what became of the basket seller. His stall stood empty at market, and the other merchants seemed to treat it as a symbol of bad luck. No one would use it to sell their goods.

Caravans began to leave the city more frequently, and several of our regular guests went with them. One or two bid us farewell before they took their families away to the cities in the east or south. Some went north, but after two moons Pharaoh sent out a decree that restricted travel into Egypt.

"My children are not safe here," I heard Politan telling Banune on his last visit to the House of Palms. "If the priests of Moloch do not kill them, then the Semites will."

"Semites will not attack the city," Banune chided. "Even if they do, what hope have they of prevailing over the king's army? They are nomads; they live in tents and herd sheep. With what do they fight? Their staffs?"

"I have seen them on my trips into the hills," he told her. "There are thousands gathering together on the other side of the river. I do not know how they will cross it, but if they do, the only thing that stands between them and the rest of Canaan is Riha."

She shook her head. "No army of sheep herders can take the city. We are safe."

Narath, who came two and three times each week, made things bearable. He arrived early to purchase a full night of mut'a, and always spent it with me.

"I should have a regular like the builder," Zakiti complained. "I would get more sleep."

While I sometimes worried that Narath could ill afford the expense, I was grateful for the time alone with him. He was an attentive and unhurried lover, and when we were not making the shakab, we talked of our days and the ordinary things that happened. I did not share nights like that with any of the other men, and I did not look forward to the day when he lost interest in me or had to move on. But I soon discovered that Narath was content with being with me and planned to remain in Meshnedef for some time.

"I have found weakness in most of the outer walls around Meshnedef," Narath told me one night, with a wry sort of satisfaction, "so it will take many months to supervise the repairs."

"I am glad." I propped myself on his bare chest and looked down at him. "Unless . . . do you miss your home?"

"I do not have one here," he confessed. "When I came to Riha, I had thought to buy a small house in the citadel, but it was easier for me to sleep and eat at an inn near the work sites."

I traced the long line of his collarbone. "You were not born here?"

"No, lovely one. I am from Hazor, to the north. My father was the master mason of that city, and trained me how to build." He rolled over so that I lay beneath him. "Where lives your family?"

"In the merchants' quarter." I curled my hand around his neck and looked into his eyes. He would understand, I thought, and decided to tell him the truth of my past. "They are not my family anymore. I was cast out."

"You? But you are so kind and thoughtful a girl." He caressed my cheek. "What made them do this to you?"

"A petty quarrel with my stepmother, which she turned to her advantage. It matters not." I shifted under him. "When you must leave here, where will you go next?"

"The king wishes me to return to the upper city now, so that I can oversee the completion of the new temple. But I have refused." His eyes darkened. "It is one thing to build up the city's defenses, and another to erect a monument to that monster of a god. I shall have nothing to do with it."

"You speak of the seventh temple of Moloch?" When he nodded, I frowned. "But the king can simply order you to work there, and you will have to go or risk being thrown into the kele." So it was with anyone who did not bow to the will of Khormad.

"Not so, for your king cannot command me. I am not one of his subjects, or even a citizen of Riha." He nuzzled my neck. "I am here on the tolerance of the king of Hazor. When my father retires, I shall return and take his place as master builder."

I did not want to think of him leaving me or Riha, and put my arms around him tightly. "I wish . . ." I stopped myself. "I hope your father will not retire for a long time."

"Knowing my father? He will be there to *build* my funeral tomb." He lifted his head and gazed down at me. "I should not jest about death. It is said that Baal is the last one to laugh at them."

I did not believe in Baal, or in knowing what the future would bring, but in that moment I felt a terrible foreboding. It left me as stricken as if I had already lost Narath.

"I have given you little sleep tonight." He was eager against me, but he asked me, considerate as always. "Are you too tired to take me again?"

I was tired and feeling out of sorts, but that was not his fault. I forced a smile to my lips and moved under him, feeling more like a harlot than I had serving other men. "Never."

When Narath left the following morning, my unhappiness lingered. Although we spent long hours together, the more often he came to me, the more the nights seemed to shrink. It seemed only a moment from the time that I greeted him to our last, affectionate embrace. I went to help Cook, who was at last back on her feet, but I could not keep my mind on the work and made clumsy mistakes.

"Rahab," she said after scolding me for dropping something a third time, "go and weave. Go milk the goats. Go to market." When I stared at her, she pointed to the door. "Go *anywhere*, but make it not my kitchen."

I went to the garden first, but I was too restless to sit and listen to the water and the palms. I paced the length of the garden, my steps so loud that two of the long-horned goats wandered over to the garden side of the enclosure to watch me.

Narath would not come again to the house for two or three days. The weather was too hot for most of the zanna to venture out. Although Tiamat had recovered from Akhete's abuse, she caught a cold and stayed in her room, only appearing downstairs now and then. Banune was constantly busy running the household and watching over Cook, who was still hobbling. I had no one to talk to, no one who could reassure me.

If Tezi were here, she would calm me.

Since spending the little time I had with Jiela, I missed my sister more keenly than ever. I wanted to speak with her, see her, and know she was well. I felt a crushing pain in my heart as I realized she still did not know my fate. I had been so involved in coping with this new life of mine that I had hardly given her feelings a single thought.

I would see her again. I would see her today.

I went back in to retrieve a cloak and told Cook I would be gone for several hours.

"By yourself?" She waggled a wooden spoon at me. "You are not supposed to go out without one of the others. It is not safe, not with the guards searching every house looking for Semite spies."

"There are no Semite spies in Riha." Given the ferocity with which they were pursued, the very idea was ridiculous.

"The king thinks there are, which of course means there are," Cook snapped. "Each day more heads are piked. It is said no man with a beard in Riha is safe anymore."

"Happily I am not a bearded man." Since I had eaten nothing since last evening, I packed the little handbasket Evora had given me with some fig cakes, a piece of lehem and some cheese, as well as a small skin of water. "I shall return before dark."

"You'd better," Cook said. "Zakiti started her moon time this morning, and Ubalnu hasn't yet finished hers. With Tia ill, if you are not here, they may start sending the men to *me* to make the shakab."

"Weigh Darbas's silver carefully," I advised her.

"His sheqels are sometimes lighter than they should be."

I was two streets away when I realized that I had never truly been alone for any significant length of time since coming to the House of Palms. I was by myself in my room, of course, and in the garden if I chose to be, or in the enclosure when I took my turn tending to the goats. Outside of those times, I remained in the company of the other zanna or the men who came to the house.

Tiamat.

It was so subtle a thing that I had not noticed it, and I could not actually prove it, but the more I thought on it, the more I was convinced she had somehow arranged to keep me from being alone.

Was it because she did not trust me? I looked down at the green scarab ring on my finger. *No, she would not have given me this if that were so.*

I walked quickly through the streets of Meshnedef, following the most direct route out of the quarter. To get to the house of my father, I had to pass through part of the artisans' quarter, where silversmiths forged fine jewelry, ceremonial weapons, and the plain ingots that would be reduced over time into the beqa, sheqel, and mina we citizens used. Here, too, there were many city guards, ever watchful, and few women, so I drew much attention. I quickened my pace and moved into the merchants' quarter.

I stopped beside a small, well-thatched brewery house, and there in the shade drank some water and ate a little lehem to settle my stomach. Another street over were the homes of the weavers, rug makers, and tailors of Riha. From here I could smell dye and wool, and feel the twisting, kinking strands against my fingers. Looms, rarely idle, were being used this moment to make more goods for market. My father would not like the ban on red dye—it was a favorite color of his—but he would accept it. Robur preferred to accept a certain amount of deprivation in exchange for a peaceful life.

Maybe that was why he was so quick to believe Helsbah's lies about me. Because to do otherwise would be too much trouble.

I shoved the water skin back into my handbasket, pulled my hood forward so that it hid my face completely, and walked across the last two streets to my bet ab, the house of my father.

It had been two months since I had left here, devastated and not caring what happened to me. For all the other years of my life, this house had been my whole world. So why did it look so small and shabby? Why were there weeds sprouting up where there had once been lush grass? Where were the servants, who should have been preparing for the return of the master from market, or baking lehem for the evening meal, or sweeping the steps at the front of the house?

A veiled woman carrying a market basket filled with gingerroot and wild onions stopped beside me. "Do you look for someone, mistress?" she asked.

I knew her voice—it was Clori, the daughter of

Kelles, the wool merchant—and she might recognize mine if I spoke. I simply shook my head.

"That is the home of Robur the Weaver." She pulled aside her veil so that I could see her face. "He is at market, if you are looking for him. Or do you seek someone else?"

It would seem I would have to speak. "I seek his daughter," I said, trying to alter my voice to be lower and deeper than it was.

"The little one is probably at her lessons. The other, well . . ." Clori paused and peered at me. "Do you know Rahab?"

"I know of her."

"It was a terrible thing. Such lies that woman told about her." The wool merchant's daughter shook her head sadly. "Not that Robur would hear the truth until long after Rahab was gone, and then it was too late. At least she is out of the house."

"The stepmother?"

"Oh, no, I mean Rahab. Robur says she made a good match with one of his cousin's sons in the city of Jirabar." Clori sighed. "Helsbah remains mistress of the house, although she is never there. Too busy dancing attendance on that brother of hers, I'd say. He was promoted to a minor ministry, but to hear her tell it you would think him crowned king."

I could not bear to hear any more about my father's lies or Helsbah's ridiculous social climbing. "I thank you." Before Clori could speak again, I walked away from her, away from my father's house, and waited around the corner until she had disappeared into her home before crossing the street.

I went to the servant's side entrance, which I expected to be answered by Old Merti, the housekeeper. Instead, a slovenly-looking younger woman I had never before seen appeared. She was the filthiest-looking slave I had ever seen, and glared at me through the greasy spikes of hair hanging over her eyes. "What is it?"

"Where is the housekeeper?" I asked without thinking.

"Old Merti? She has been sold, with the others." The woman wiped her wet hands down the front of her robe, leaving new stains atop the old ones. "I am the housekeeper."

"You?" She was not fit to look after the animals.

"Yes, me." Her expression turned impatient. "What do you want? I am busy."

Think before you act. I looked down at the basket in my hand. "I am sent with a gift for young Tezi from Clori, daughter of Kelles." The housekeeper held out her hand. "My mistress begs me present it with a personal message to the young lady."

"Oh, very well." She let me in and pointed in the direction of Tezi's bedchamber. "She is sulking in there. Tell her that if she does not eat her afternoon meal, her father will shout at me, and I shall beat her."

Trembling, I walked down the hall and past my old room. Tezi's door was closed, and she did not answer when I tapped on it. I slipped inside.

My little sister lay on her sleeping mat, her favorite coverlet clutched around her despite the heat of the day. She was staring at nothing, and did not look up at me as she said, "I do not feel well. Go away."

I pulled off my veil. "Is this how you get out of your lessons? Making a pretense of sickness?"

The sound of my voice made Tezi cry out and jump to her feet. "Rabi?"

I nodded and held out my arms, which a moment later were filled with my small, sobbing sister.

I did not dare stay long with Tezi. The housekeeper would have become suspicious, and I was loath to stay when Helsbah or my father might return at any moment.

"What happened to all of the servants?" I asked her.

"Father had to sell most of them. He does not do well at market now." Tezi frowned. "No one skilled will work for what he offers, and you know that he cannot weave as well as you did."

So my father had suffered my absence, too. It was a curious kind of justice, but I could not rejoice in it. "What of Helsbah?"

"Little Mother hardly comes home at all. She spends her days at Uncle's home in the citadel. When she is here, she complains without cease." My sister wrapped her arms around me. "Oh, Rabi, I have been so lonely without you. I tried to pray, as you taught me, but Jehovah does not listen. Or He did not until today."

"Father would be very angry if he found me here, and Little Mother . . ." I could only imagine what Helsbah would do. As I was cast out of the family, I had no right to be in the house. She might even have me arrested and sent to the kele for trespassing. "I must go now, but I shall come and see you again."

"But where do you go? How are you living?" She eyed my wig. "Are you married? Is he handsome? Can I come and live with you?"

That last question nearly broke my heart. "Tezi, listen to me." I smoothed the hair back from her face. "I am safe where I am, and that is all that matters. Someday things will be so that you may come and visit me. Until then, you must stay with Father."

"He pays no mind to me. It is as if I am not even here." Her face clouded. "I want to be with you, Rabi."

"I want that, too, Little Sister, but it cannot be." I heard footsteps in the corridor outside and disentangled myself from her embrace. "I shall come to see you again as soon as I can. Remember me in your prayers." As the door to her room opened behind me, I quickly handed her the basket. "My mistress thanks you for the many hesed you have given her."

Tezi frowned and then looked past me. "What is it?"

"It is time for your meal." The housekeeper gave me a suspicious look. "As for you, you should get back to your house."

I bowed to the housekeeper and Tezi, who looked as if she might hurl herself at me again. Then she

nodded, and I left the room quickly without looking back.

The hour was not yet too late, I decided as I went
outside. I still had time to make one more visit before
I returned to the House of Palms.

The market in Meshnedef where I shopped with
the other zanna was truly pitiful compared to the
larger, king's marketplace near the citadel. There my
father and other well-to-do merchants kept permanent shops and sold their goods to the wealthier citizens of Riha. Of course, I had as much business going
there as I did visiting Tezi, but after what my sister
had told me, I had to see just how bad things were
for Robur.

My father's shop was open, but there were no rugs
or cloth bolts on display near the windows. The steps
to the shop had not been swept in many weeks, and
I saw no patrons going in or coming out.

There was no sign of my father, either.

I could stand outside and wonder, or I could go
in and face him. Being outcast did not prevent me
from being a patron, in my view, and I wanted to
see him. I wanted to know that what Tezi said was
true, and that he had endured a little of what I had.
I wanted to know why he wasn't taking better care
of the only daughter he had left, as well.

I walked slowly into the shop. The bareness of the
shelves startled me, for Robur had always kept a
good stock. What he had out was not my work, and
of such poor quality that I doubted he could have
sold it in Meshnedef. The loom in the back of the

shop was also silent, not a good sign. My father had always employed an apprentice to whom he taught weaving and rug repair, which kept the loom busy all day.

I was the greater part of the reason my father had prospered, for Robur did not have to pay a daughter to weave for him. Perhaps with the way things were, he would welcome me back.

And when he asks how you have been living, as your sister did? A coldness twisted inside me. *How will you answer him? Do you imagine Robur the Weaver would permit a common harlot to live under his roof, even if she had once been his daughter?*

"May I show you something, mistress?" my father asked as he stepped out of the shop's back workroom.

I could not believe the change in him. He looked ten years older than the last time I had seen him, with more white in his hair and a shabbiness to his garments that was just as disturbing. Above all things, my father had always taken pride in his appearance.

I thought of doing as I had with Clori, but now it seemed a ridiculous thing. This was my father. I had loved him all my life. I pulled back my veil to expose my face. "Greetings, Father."

"Rahab." He took the sight of me as he would a blow, and could not speak for a long time. "Why did you come here?"

"Many reasons." I watched the emotions play over his tired face. "One to send a message to your wife, the lying bitch. Tell her that I did not die in the gutter, as she hoped."

"You will not speak of Helsbah," he grated. "She was deeply wounded by what you did to her."

"Yes, I imagine she suffered to no end." I would not feel a drop of pity for Robur. "Yet somehow she finds it in her ability to leave my sister alone in an empty house with only a slatternly slut to look after her. Or was that your doing, Father?"

"Many have suffered because of your treachery." He flung a hand out. "Look at my shop. Look what you have done to me."

"What *I* have done? Did *I* shave my own head? Did I throw myself out into the street?" I came toward him, my hands in tight fists. "Did *I* ignore the truth? Did I once in my entire *life* give you reason to think I would do such terrible things to Helsbah, or any other person, for that matter?"

He looked uncomfortable for a moment. "People change. She showed me the evidence of your evil."

"Oh, Father. She *invented* the evidence."

He folded his arms. "I had to protect the honor of my name, and my family."

"Well, you did so, and now you will starve for it. But know this." I held up my hand when he would have spoken again. "When Helsbah leaves you, and you face being thrown out into the street, I shall come. I shall come for my sister and take her away from you."

"You cannot have Tezi."

I made a disgusted sound. "You would let her

starve? You would sell her into slavery? How will you care for her when everything is gone?"

"What of you, Daughter?" he countered. "How do you make your way without kin to help you? Are you a thief now? A beggar? How could you support your sister?"

"Very well." I smiled, a cold, terrible smile. "I have become a harlot, Father." He flinched back, appalled. "Better than a thief or a beggar, would you not say? I serve in a house of harlots in Meshnedef. That is where I shall take Tezi. I think she will make a fine harlot. Just as I have."

His face turned dark. "Never. I shall never permit it."

"That is what happens to women who have no one to care for them." I leaned close to him. "Find a new weaver, sell more rugs, do whatever you must to take better care of my sister. Or you will be the only merchant in Riha who can claim two whores for daughters."

He slapped me. "Get out of my shop."

I touched my throbbing cheek. "Yes, I think I shall. Farewell, Father. Do not forget what I have said."

CHAPTER

9

I did not hurry as I walked out of my father's shop. I wanted to savor my victory. I wanted to brand the pain of it upon my heart, so that I would never forget. The day was still young, I did not have to run back to Meshnedef. I could shop here, in the king's marketplace. I could buy something for Tiamat. I could do whatever I wished. I did not have to return to the House of Palms.

It struck me then: for all of Tiamat's kindness, for all I owed to Banune and the others for teaching me how to make my way in the world, I did not wish to go back. Not even to be with Narath again.

Life as a harlot was all I had, but in that moment, it became unbearable to me.

Despite my words to my father, I wanted to turn and hurry back to his shop and beg his forgiveness. Or I might go home and be with my sister again. I could wait there for Robur, and when he came home, drop on my knees and plead with him to make me family again. I wanted this even as I knew there was no possibility of it.

After what I had said to my father, I may have saved Tezi, but I had forever destroyed any chance of regaining my old life.

I walked slowly through the streets of my old quarter, and noticed something different. This time of day, there were always children about, the older coming home from their lessons, the younger playing in the outer courtyards. They were always noisy about it, and yet I saw and heard no children at all. Then I saw the permanent shutters over a row of windows, indicating the house they belonged to was closed and uninhabited. So, too, was the next one, and two houses from that, another shuttered dwelling.

By the time I left the merchants' quarter, I had counted more that thirty dwellings that were shuttered and stood empty. Abandoned houses in a quarter where families lived for many generations.

I was so preoccupied with this startling realization that I did not watch where I was walking. When two men crossed my path, I blundered directly into the taller of the pair.

"Kiatta immadi." His hands grasped my waist briefly, and then dropped away. "I beg your pardon, mistress."

I stared up at him in horror. I knew that phrase. "What did you say?"

"Nothing. He said nothing." The shorter man nudged his companion. "Let us go."

I could not permit them to pass. "You said 'kiatta immadi,'" I said to the first man.

He muttered something under his breath before he made a dismissive gesture. "No, you did not hear me correctly." He had a beautiful, mellow voice that, under different circumstances, I might never tire of hearing. "It was something else."

Such a wonderful voice, and he was using it to lie to me.

"I know what I heard, and what it means." It was something my mother uttered frequently during her prayers to Jehovah. It was a *Semite* phrase. "'For you are with me.'"

The tall man looked from side to side before seizing my arm and leading me around a corner. Then he pulled back his hood and revealed his face.

He had dark green eyes and straight black hair, not so different from many Canaanite men whose tribal ancestors came from the north and east. A few had the same narrow, tilted eye shape as he. This man too was clean-shaven, like any man of Riha, but judging by the pale skin on his jaw and chin, only recently.

Something about him made me go very still—the eyes, perhaps. There was a quality in them that made me think of the hokhmah nisteret, the wisdom hidden from plain sight. Or the way he gazed down at me, as if he, too, was wary of something in my own. I did not know this man, had never seen him, and had never heard his voice. I could say that without doubt. So why did I feel as if I had been looking for him without knowing? Why was there this sense of relief welling up in me?

"How do you know He who is with us, mistress?" he asked me.

Horror welled up in me. Why was I talking to this man as I only had to my mother? He was a stranger. He was nothing to me.

"It matters not." Even if he were Semite, I did not dare trust him with my secrets. He could leave here; I could not. "The king has his men out looking for spies. Strangers to the city are detained and questioned. By your very presence, you risk arrest."

"You are mistaken, mistress, for we are but traders from the south," the shorter man said, his voice harsh. "Come, Salme, we must go if we are to finish our walk before sunset."

Traders from the south, when they wore nothing suitable for crossing the desert, and had skin the color of goat's milk. Idiot men.

"You need better lies," I snapped. "Anyone who looks at you can tell you are not from the south; you are too pale. Desert traders spend their whole lives crossing back and forth over the Negev and look as if made of copper. You should have shaved off your beards long before you came here, too."

The one called Salme rubbed a hand against the side of his face. "It is that obvious."

"A child would notice it." I knew of some cosmetics that would help, but I doubted men would elect to use them. "Rub some dirt into your skin; it will disguise the pale places. Keep your face in the sun when you can without being seen to even out the color. And only speak Canaanite; the guards will arrest you the moment they hear anything else out of your mouth."

The shorter man scowled and drew a dagger. "How do we know you will not betray us?"

"Because if I wanted to," I whispered furiously, "I would have screamed for the city guards the moment I heard your friend praise the presence of Him in our lives."

"She tells the truth, Yofni," Salme said. He did not smile at me, but his eyes changed, and he caught one of my hands between his. "I would thank you for the advice, but I do not know your name."

Later I would think of Narath, and feel shame for how I looked up at Salme. Later I would cringe at the wantonness of it, of seeing myself in his eyes. Of wishing I was still Rahab, daughter of Robur, a girl who could weave and make her little sister laugh and stand up to a bully like Helsbah.

But I was not that girl anymore. I was Rahab the Harlot, and the only business I had with men was conducted in private and paid for with silver.

"It does not matter. Get out of Riha before you are killed." I turned and hurried away.

"It is ridiculous," Narath said to me several nights later. "The king asks the impossible of me. I cannot do it."

I straddled his back and poured a little scented oil

on my hands before I began working it into his taut muscles. Banune had suggested giving my master builder a massage when he was tense, as it was something men who toiled many hours enjoyed. "Can you not tell the king so? You said that he could not command you."

"These are days when one does not deny Khormad easily." He groaned as my hands reached his shoulders. "There, yes, that is the worst of it. Your touch is magic, Rahab."

I gentled my fingers. "So what is it the king wishes of you now?"

"He refuses to let me do the proper repair work on the outer walls," Narath said. "I am directed to build atop the old walls already, and they have fallen too many times to count. Many years of tremors have riddled the slopes and grounds around the city with hidden chasms and cavities. Too many are near the walls."

I had never heard this about Riha. Walls collapsed now and then, but they were always quickly repaired. "Can you not fill in the gaps?"

"I do, but the king has my men using sand instead of plaster or gravel. Soil is not enough, I tell him, but does he listen to me? No." He sighed. "So the walls I repair remain as sturdy as those a child might make of sticking pebbles in dirt."

I thought of the wall looming behind the House of Palms. If it were to fall inward . . . "Have you told him this? Does he not see how dangerous it is?"

"I have, several times. The king is obsessed with

the cult of Moloch and says the temples are more important. While he has his goldsmiths gilding every godhead in the city, the walls and battlements that keep out invaders begin to crumble." He turned his head to look at me. "Do not worry. It is not quite as bad as I make it out. I am like my father and want perfection in all things."

"As you say." What he said troubled me, though. Riha depended heavily on the walls that had always kept out invaders. If they did fall, there would be nothing to prevent the city from being overrun.

I thought of the two Semites I had chanced upon after leaving my father's shop. Salme and Yofni had been sent to Riha for a reason. Was it as spies, to learn of the city's defenses? Did the Semites intend to attack?

Narath turned under me and caught my hands, bringing them to his chest. "Ah, I have upset you. Never worry, lovely one. I shall keep you and the zanna safe."

Despite Narath's assurances, I did not sleep well that night, and only picked at my meal the next morning. I returned as soon as I could to my room, hoping to lose my worries while weaving.

The wool I had chosen to use for the weft was the widest and softest of the skeins Tiamat had given me. The fullness of it suited the thinner warp as well as my weave pattern, while the easy texture allowed me to use the weft from the skein itself without fear of tangling it. The combination would make the finished cloth pleasing to touch and very strong.

I picked up the shed stick I had fashioned from a peeled oak twig, and threaded it through the warp above the highest crossings of the thread. Pulling the rod down, I opened the shed, the space for the next pass of the weft ball.

Jezere said that she could see patterns hanging in the space between the threads, waiting to be discovered, that had never been made on a loom. Each thread was a life, and how it crossed and wove itself into another made it weaker or stronger.

If I was the warp, were the zanna my weft? Or was I theirs?

I passed the skein of weft thread through the shed from where I had left off weaving, left to right, and wound it around the right post to hold it in place. I picked up another stick I had broken in two lengthwise—I would need to see Cook about finding a long, flat bone to make a proper tamper—and worked it through the tighter warp threads, making the second shed for the right-to-left pass of the weft.

I could not see patterns that had not been worked, as my mother had, but I could see how lives meshed together. Narath had become a strong foundation thread in my life. Tiamat and the other zanna wove their different personalities around me, too. I could see them as colors: Tiamat's liveliness made her a deep green, Banune's compassion and practicality a warm amber, Karasbaal's abrasiveness a jarring yellow, Cook's grumbling and ceaseless toils a sturdy gray. Zakiti's love of admiration could be brilliant orange or flaring purple, while Arwia's perpetual serenity invoked a placid blue. I could not think of Ubalnu as anything but the black of night, but even that had its place on the loom.

What was my color? Was I, as Tia had said, suited to the vibrancy of red? If so, why was my color the same as blood? The same as the god Moloch's? What did it mean?

I pulled the weft too sharply and had to adjust it before I tied it to the left post. With my fingers, I pushed down the two new rows of weave.

It was silly to be worried about myself when so much was happening around Riha. Narath had not been sent to repair the walls for nothing, and each day the city guards were out looking for Semites to arrest or kill.

My mother had told me that Canaan was the land Jehovah had promised to the Semites when they had gone out of Egypt. And while it had been more than forty years since my mother's people had escaped the oppression and slavery under Pharaoh, they had not come into Canaan, but lived as wandering nomads in the wilderness to the north.

Someday Jehovah will deliver Canaan into the hands of our people, Jezere had told me. *When they are ready, He will cause them to come down from the mountains. Their army will cross the river and take that which belongs to them. Nothing and no one will stand in their way, for they are the children of the One and True God. This will come to pass, and soon, so you and Tezi must be prepared.*

137

She had never told me how to prepare. She had only told me that when the time came, I would know what to do.

"Rahab."

I looked up to see Banune standing with clean linens and a jug of water. "What is it?"

"I knocked, but you did not hear me. I need you to help me."

I took the jug of water and followed her to Tiamat's room. "I thought she was feeling better."

"She has been deceiving all of us." Banune did not knock on Tia's door but walked in. To me, she said, "Lower the shades, and light the oil lamps."

I did so, but when I went over to the bed, the sight of Tiamat nearly made me stumble. The beautiful woman who had done so much for me and the other zanna had been reduced to a mere shadow of herself, thin and ashen-faced. Sweat was rolling off her skin and she was not fully conscious. Banune pulled back the coverlet and parted Tiamat's robe.

"What is wrong with her?" I picked up Tia's limp hand and held it.

"It is a fever spell. She has them now and again." Banune gently sponged the sweat from Tia's legs and gently placed her hand on her brow. Even that slight pressure made Tia groan. "They have never been so bad as this, or lasted so long."

I knew nothing of fevers, except that they were dangerous. "Will she live?"

"I cannot say." Banune lowered her robe. "Can

you lift her for me, so that I may put fresh linen beneath her?"

As gently as I could, I put my arms under Tiamat's knees and neck and lifted her. It was as if she weighed no more than Tezi now, and her body felt as hot as lehem fresh from the oven. She stiffened and moaned, and then opened her eyes to look up at me.

"Rahab." She tried to smile.

"So this is why you are not downstairs, stealing the men away from us." I saw the terrible weariness in her eyes, which were dull and bloodshot. "We will summon the healer."

"No. I have seen him before and he can do nothing for me. It is an old sickness, with no remedy." Tiamat tried to lift her hand and then sighed. "When the fever comes, I am like a baby. I have put your red wig to soak in the last of my henna." She glanced at a small pail beneath the vanity. "Dry it well before you wear it again. Do you know, you never told me why your mother named you Rahab."

Banune met my gaze and bit her lip.

"My mother had a vast amount of trouble birthing me," I told her. "My shoulders were so wide that I became stuck, halfway born. The midwife had to put oil on them to help me come into the world."

"The gods must have known how much weight you would bear upon them, to fashion you so. I am glad. I am so tired." Her head lolled back on my arm.

I looked at Banune, who had changed the linens

on the bed and nodded, and then carefully lowered Tiamat back down.

Banune rested a hand on her forehead. "I shall stay with her. Say nothing to the others if you can help it. She would not want them to know she is this ill. Can you manage things downstairs?"

"Yes." Ubalnu would not like me taking charge, but the others would raise no objections. "There is nothing else we may do for her?"

"I have heard you praying to your One God," she said. "Perhaps you would ask Him to save her."

I felt my throat go tight, but I saw no hatred in her eyes, and nodded before I left them.

As usual, Karasbaal was the first downstairs that evening, but when he saw me setting up the great room for the night, he came in to question me. "Where are Tiamat and Banune?"

"They both have their moon time," I said, lining up the goblets to be filled with wine. "I shall see to the guests tonight."

"You, the little novice? How far you have come in so short a time." He caught my arm in a strong grip and made me face him. He had bleached his hair again, only too much this time, which had given it a greenish yellow tinge. "Only one of them could have a moon time."

"What?"

"Tiamat does not bleed; she is barren." He glanced over his shoulder. "Now, tell me the truth of it."

"She is having a fever spell. Banune is looking

after her, and asked me to manage for the night." I looked up into his painted eyes. Even with the cosmetics he wore to maintain his charade, I could not think of him as a woman. "Will you let go of me?"

His grasp became an odd caress. "One of the women who hires me prefers the ayin-yada, and she would gladly pay more to watch two instead of one. You could come with me some night."

"Make the shakab with you? In front of some bulge-eyed woman?" I shook my head. "I thank you, no. I am better suited to other things."

"Ah, yes, I forgot. You specialize in serving stump-faced stone pilers." Karasbaal made a rude gesture. "He will tire of you soon enough, Rahab. They always do. Then what will you do for your tiph'eret?"

"I am not doing this for pleasure," I told him.

"Once you have a true taste of what can be done, you will." He laughed. "When Ubalnu does not get enough from her men, she creeps into my room and begs me take her. Did you guess it? That is why she hates me, because she cannot bring me to my knees like the others. So she crawls to me instead."

That explained why they treated each other with such contempt—to hide their shame—but not why he was telling me. I became uneasy. "You should not do that to her."

"As long as I beat her before I take her, she likes it well enough," he assured me, his voice becoming curiously toneless. "Much in the same way she did when she was a girl, and her father and brothers made use of her."

Whatever innocence I had left vanished in that instant. I looked away from his face to see Ubalnu standing just behind us. Karasbaal had his back to her, so he was unaware of her presence. From her expression she must have heard every word he had uttered. She held her head down so that I could not see her eyes, and a moment later she was gone, as silently as she had appeared.

Instead of shame or revulsion, I felt a deep, weary sadness. "I cannot go with you, Karasbaal. I am not like Ubalnu. You should not say such things about her, or yourself."

"You refuse me?" He was astonished. "When you would spread your legs for any man in Riha with enough silver to pay your price? Is that what I must do? Buy you for myself?" He began to fumble with the purse tied to his waist. "How much, Rahab?"

"I regret that I cannot lie with you," I said quietly. "Not for any amount."

His face twisted, and he shoved me away from him. "Someday you will need me, you little bitch. I shall remember this when that time comes, and teach you what regret truly is." He stalked out of the house.

CHAPTER

10

I went out to the stairs, intending to go up to speak to Ubalnu, but I heard a strange sound coming from the kitchen. I followed it, and saw the dark-haired beauty working the quern stone, scraping it back and forth over some broken kernels and a wide swath of emmer flour.

I had never seen Ubalnu grinding grain, but as it was something I did when I most needed to exercise my frustrations, I understood her effort. The sack on the quern table was empty, so I went into the pantry and brought out another.

I set the sack within her reach. "Cook will be happy to see all the new flour. She hates having to make it herself."

"I did not crawl to him," Ubalnu told the stone. Although all the grain on it was now powdered, her hands continued to move without cease. "I never would. I *never* crawl."

"I know." I opened the sack and tossed a handful

of grain before the rolling stone in her hands. "He should not have said that."

"I told him in a moment of weakness and he swore he would never tell anyone." She attacked the new grain with renewed ferocity. "Not even Tiamat. He swore to me. Swore."

"He was too angry to think." Or had he known she was listening?

"He thinks I am enthralled by him." She grabbed a handful of grain from the sack and added it to the stone, making kernels fly from both sides. "Never mind. When he sleeps again, I shall go to him."

Had he not done enough to her with his cruel words? "You need not do that."

"I shall go to him," she said, as if she had not heard me, "and take my best dagger—the one Tiamat gave me when I first came here—and cut that lying tongue out of his head. Or perhaps something lower. Then we will see if the matrons of the citadel want him to decorate their bedchambers."

Her voice was growing louder, and there was grain all over the floor. "Ubalnu, stop this." I put my hands over hers to halt the motion of the stone. "Stop," I said, more gently.

"You shall tell the others." She wouldn't look at me. "They have longed to see me humiliated. They will laugh and say it is a good joke, that my own family turned me into a harlot."

"Never," I promised her. "I shall keep your secrets."

"The other girls in my village knew, and they

told," Ubalnu said to me. "Their fathers came to our house at night. They gave my father money to have me. My mother had been sold as a slave to pay my grandfather's debts, so she was gone. There were no other women in the house. I tried to fight them, but they were too strong, and too many. I could kill him for telling you."

"Karasbaal wanted to scare me, and hurt you," I said slowly. "He is bitter about his own suffering. I do not know what can be done to make the pain of it go away, for I carry my own. I only know that hurting someone because we were once hurt is not the way."

She gave me a look that chilled me to the bone. "You are free with your advice, so I shall give you some in return: do not trust me or Karasbaal, ever. He will hurt you because you deny him." Her lips parted over a feral smile. "I shall hurt you because it is the only thing besides Karasbaal that gives me pleasure."

"No, you will not," I insisted.

"How can you say that?" she shouted.

"Because you are not like him, or your father," I said. "You know what they do not."

A pounding at the front door of the house prevented Ubalnu from replying. I went to answer it and was pushed aside by four city guards who filed in, their curved khopesh drawn, their eyes moving over everything in sight.

I met the gaze of the oldest guard. "Why are you here? What do you want?"

"By the king's command, we inspect this house and its contents," he said, and showed me a papyrus scroll with Khormad's seal affixed to it. "You, harlot, will stand aside or be taken to the kele for interfering with our search."

Evora and the children were long gone, so it could not be for them. Nothing else could have brought them here. "What do you seek?"

He looked down at me. "Semite spies."

"Here?" I gestured around me. "In this house? Do you not know where you are, master?"

"You are whores; Semites are the sons of whores." The guard sneered at me. "Perhaps they come to make the shakab with their mothers."

"You have no cause to say such things." I straightened my back. "Ours is a respectable business. We are known to many in this quarter and we cause no trouble. To accuse us of harboring spies is unreasonable."

"I do not need a reason," he warned me. "All I need do is find one Semite here, and your pretty little painted heads will be lining the battlements first thing in the morning."

I was ordered to be silent and stay where I was, so there was no chance for me to warn Banune or any of the others. The men went through the house like the khamsin, knocking over furniture, scattering belongings, and jerking open doors. I thought of Ubalnu in the kitchen, how angry she was, and prayed she would not take out her temper on the guards.

They found nothing, of course, but through the window I saw some of our regular guests approaching the house. When the oldest guard returned to the first floor, I beckoned to him.

He came over, his face dark with suspicion and dislike. "What is it?"

"Our guests begin to arrive," I told him. As if to emphasize my words, the bell outside clanged. "I would know if they are permitted to come into the house, or if I should turn them away."

"Let them in." He seized the sleeve of my robe and brought the sharp tip of his javelin close to my face. I flinched as he tapped my cheek with the edge. "One at a time."

I nodded and tried to hide my trembling as I went to the door. Outside stood Hlavat, the old scribe, who looked puzzled.

"Is something wrong?" he whispered, trying to see past me. "Why are there guards in the house?"

"They are searching for spies," I murmured. In a louder voice I said, "Yes, master, I am happy to see you again. Please come in."

Hlavat walked in and immediately faced the oldest guard. Instead of cowering, he grinned. "Tashish, you oversized mule, what do you here?"

"Master Hlavat." The oldest guard gave him casual salute. "The king sends us to search this privy of a quarter. Spies are known to frequent such places, and there are a dozen or more hiding in the city. Why do you come here?"

"Why else does a man come to visit harlots? Not

to talk about the weather," the old scribe joked. "You have to admit, the House of Palms has some of the loveliest women in Riha."

"That one looks clean enough." Tashish eyed me the same way he might a tasty haunch of roasted meat. "Have you used her? Is she any good?"

I closed my eyes for a moment to block out his face and the fact that he would ask such things in front of mine. He was a city guard, and while none had ever come to the House of Palms during my stay, I knew such men could not be turned away. If he wanted me, I would have to take him to my room.

"That one I cannot recommend," Hlavat said, shaking his head a little. "She has no real skill, and when I make the shakab with her, she but sighs and twitches. A man wants more than a limp rag in his arms."

I had never been with Hlavat, as he would have no one but Arwia. He was lying to protect me by making Tashish think me unappealing. I held my tongue and looked at the floor as if chastened by his false claim.

Tashish cuffed the scribe's shoulder. "You should pay her a little more, old man. More silver always gets their hips moving."

I saw the other guards descending the stairs. In their arms they carried bundles of robes, coverlets and rugs, as well as other personal belongings. I knew the city guard often helped themselves to whatever they wanted, but I couldn't help the distressed sound that came when I saw the red robes Tiamat had given me, as well as the weavings from her loom and my own. From the look of the cut, hanging threads, they had used their khopesh to hack them off the looms.

Tashish looked at his men, and then at me. "Red is banned for the use of anyone except the priests of Moloch, harlot. You should remember this."

Lukur again. Would he not rest until he had taken every bit of red from the world? I managed a nod.

Hlavat saw the guards out, and when they had departed, gave me a sympathetic look. "The king must be desperate if he is looking for spies in Meshnedef."

I thought of Salme and Yofni, and how they had so freely walked the streets of the merchants' quarter. With all the shuttered houses there, perhaps they were hiding in one. I sent a brief prayer to Jehovah and asked him to watch over the Semites—and to get them out of Riha before the likes of Tashish discovered them.

I saw that the old scribe was watching me closer than I had imagined, so I shrugged. "Spies could not chance dallying with harlots."

"You would know they were Semites the moment they took off their robes," he said. At my blank look, he added, "Since leaving Egypt, Semites have engaged in a curious practice. They cut off a piece of their male children's foreskins when they are born."

My mother had told me this—circumcision, she

had called it, as part of a covenant with Jehovah—
but I had to pretend not to know. "That sounds
very painful."

"That is my thinking. Another reason to be glad
not to be born Semite." His expression grew serious.
You did well not to challenge the guard, Rahab. Tashish and his kind would not hesitate to skewer anyone who gets in their way. Never cross the will of
the guard, for it is the will of the king."

"You did not have much difficulty with them," I
said, not sure how I felt about the old scribe's ease
in dealing with such men.

"I was a favorite of Khormad's father, the king
before, and I took pains not to make any enemies at
court while I served him." He smiled a little. "Do
you know, Tashish was a house slave in those days.
He plied a fan to keep flies off the queen and emptied the royal privy pots."

I thought of my weaving, and Tiamat's. "Now he
terrifies and steals from the innocent. He has come
up in the world."

"Dear girl." He came over and clasped my hands.
"I am sorry about them taking your things. There
was no argument I could make against it. This ban
on red, the madness with Moloch, and the gate inspections have us all questioning the king's reason."

"Gate inspections?" I had never heard of this.

"Khormad believes Semites are disguising themselves as traders and travelers in order to gain access
to the city. He has posted permanent inspectors at
every point in and out of Riha. Everyone who at-

tempts to pass through them must present a name voucher like this one"—he took out a small baked-clay square marked with the impression of an official's seal—"and still they are searched."

I remembered Salme's pale but handsome face, and wondered how long it would be before I saw it again atop a pike on the wall.

"I have frightened you," the old man said, taking my arm. "Forgive me."

"Oh, no, I am well." There was nothing to be done about Salme or Yofni, and I had responsibilities to look after here. "Come and have a glass of wine. I know Arwia is anxious to see you."

Somehow Banune nursed Tiamat through the terrible fever spell, and several days later she was well enough to come downstairs for the morning meal. The other zanna, who had not known how seriously ill she had been, were shocked at the sight of her.

"I am fine," Tiamat told them, waving her hands and smiling. "Hungry, too. I shall have a bowl of your milk and wheat, Cook, and some fruit."

Cook brought the bowl over herself, making a great show of thumping it down and scowling. "Next you will have me washing your feet and painting your face, I suppose." She fussed with the fruit basket, picking through it herself to find the choicest dates and figs for Tia.

"If you propose to be a body servant, you can serve me," Ubalnu said. "My toenails need trimming."

"So does your tongue," Karasbaal said.

I looked quickly at Ubalnu, who had a knife in her hand and was using it to slice up a piece of fruit. Her hand went still, and she looked down at the blade for a long moment before she gazed back at Karasbaal.

"I can think of many things that need such attention," she said, her tone sweet. "But the task is hardly difficult. It can be done at any hour, even when the one in need of trimming is soundly sleeping."

"Alas, I am a light sleeper." Karasbaal pushed aside the rest of his meal and rose from the table. "One should remember that."

Ubalnu watched him leave. "So I shall," I heard her mutter.

Unaware of the underlying meaning of the exchange, Banune sat down beside me. She looked tired, but spent more time watching Tiamat than eating. The effort of coming down seemed to have drained Tia's strength, for she returned to her room after only taking a few mouthfuls.

"Can you go to market today?" Banune asked me, her voice low.

"Yes, of course." Arwia had just gone the other day, however, and I knew of nothing needed for the household. "What shall I buy?"

"Take the cart and the mule, and see if the flax seller has anything in bright colors. Bring back some bundles of young stems, too. I shall soak them and spin more thread as Tia needs it." She passed a heavy pouch under the table to me. "She is too weak to do more than sit up a few hours. She will be happier with her hands busy."

I remembered how the soldiers had callously cut away the beautiful weaving from her loom. They must have taken her flax, too. "I shall see to it."

Given the conversation over our morning meal, I was loath to leave Ubalnu and Karasbaal in the house together, but I could not see how to keep them apart. Although Ubalnu disliked going to market, I decided to ask her to accompany me.

"It will not take long," I assured her after all the other zanna had left the kitchen. "An hour at the most."

"That is an hour too long." She nibbled on a slice of pomegranate. "Go by yourself."

"I do not like going alone, and I have never driven the cart," I said. "The mule does not like me, I think."

"Then take Arwia or Zakiti." She pretended to smother a yawn. "Going to market bores me."

What did not? I decided to tell her the truth. "When the city guard searched the house, they cut down Tiamat's weaving and stole it," I told her. "Banune wishes me to buy more thread and flax stems so she can start again. It will help keep her mind occupied."

"Do you think I care how Tiamat feels?" Ubalnu demanded.

"Yes," I said. "You will not admit it, but I know you do."

She gave me a nasty smile. "Have a care, Unwanted One. Soon you will imagine us all having tender feelings."

"Do this for me," I said, holding onto my temper, "and I shall owe you a favor."

"Yes, you would. I suppose I should go, if for nothing but to keep you from overturning the cart in the middle of the street." She rose from the table and stretched. "Very well, let us go and buy flax."

The marketplace was crowded, and so I tied up the mule at the entrance to the first row of stalls and left Ubalnu with the cart.

"I shall have the flax seller bring it here."

"Make it quick," she said, covering her head with her veil. "It is hot, and the flies are beginning to swarm."

The flax seller was an old Egyptian caravaneer who had settled in Riha, and now sent his sons to make the long journeys back to his homeland to buy flax. He grumbled about this, and the dangers of the hapiru raiders to the north as he sorted out a selection of flax thread for me.

"The king sends men to guard his tribute caravans, but does he protect the merchants? No." He scooped up a bundle of flax stems and placed them beside the linen thread I was examining. "Three times my shipments have been robbed this season. If this continues, my prices will be so high that Khormad himself will not be able to afford linen."

I selected the best of the dyed linen thread, and five bundles of the stems. Making the thread was an arduous task, but Banune had been so insistent.

"I have a cart at the market entrance, but it is too crowded for me to drive it back here," I told the old man. "Do you have a barrow I can use?"

"My nephew will bring it out to your cart, mistress," the flax seller said, gesturing to a healthy-looking young man winding spools at the back of the stall.

"I thank you." Since his stall was very close to that of the basket seller's, I lowered my voice and asked, "Do you know what became of the man who spoke out against the high priest?" I nodded toward the now empty stall.

"Jela?" The old man eyed me. "He was punished as is appropriate under the holy laws of the king."

"I imagine he was," I countered, "but that does not tell me what happened to him." When the flax seller hesitated, I added, "I think his wife and daughters, were they able to get word, would wish to know his fate."

He nodded his understanding. "Lord Lukur's men could not find the wife and children, so they arrested Jela and took him up to the kele at the citadel. When one of the wine merchants made a delivery near the new temple site, he said he saw Jela's body tied to the asherim. His throat had been cut, so it was quick. No one will go near his stall or his house, of course; bad luck to take the place of a dead man."

155

The small, pinched face of Jiela, who had only wanted her father to have some of Cook's stew, came into my mind. "The temple is finished, then?"

The flax seller shook his head. "Lord Lukur adds more to it daily. He is gathering up qedesh for the dedication ceremony, when he intends to sacrifice a hundred young ones to the glory of Moloch." His voice dropped to a mere whisper. "They say he is as mad as the king, and I begin to believe it."

One hundred children. My stomach turned. "Can nothing be done to prevent this?"

"No man may evade the scales of justice forever, mistress," the old man assured me. "After his body dies, his soul will be weighed in the afterlife. That one is so bloated with evil that I know the gods will immediately feed his soul to Anubis."

The dire prediction did not comfort me, and as I bid the flax seller farewell, my heart grew heavy. How many more atrocities would be committed in the name of Moloch? Why wasn't anyone doing anything to stop him or the king? Had the people of Riha become completely indifferent to the evil in their midst?

A man blocked my path, and when I tried to go around him, he stepped in front of me again. I looked up into dark green eyes and a familiar face.

"For you are with me again," he said.

CHAPTER
11

I could not believe my eyes. It was him, the tall Semite I had met in the merchants' quarter. "Salme."

He smiled. "You remember my name."

I remembered everything about him, although I had hoped to forget it. "What are you doing here?"

"Meeting my cousin, Yofni." He glanced around us. "Who is late again. You never told me your name, mistress."

"It is Rahab." I saw a group of guards entering the market and produced a bright smile, tilting my head so that it could be seen by all around us. "Guards, behind you. Do exactly as I say, right this moment, or you are a dead man."

He did not panic or make any sudden movements, but his eyes became slits. "How many?"

"Five or six." I looped my arm through his and led him to a space between two stalls. A house sat behind them, and there was a stretch of wall against

which I stood. I pulled him close before me, position-
ing him so that only his back could be seen by anyone looking at us.

He went along with me, although clearly puzzled
by my actions. "What do we here?"

"I am a harlot, and you are propositioning me," I
murmured. I had to make it appear as if we were
engaged in an intimate moment, so I tugged back
my veil and exposed my throat. "Bend over a little.
Make it seem as if you are admiring me."

"Yofni is late, but he will be here soon," he said.
"I must try to warn him." He began to look back.

I caught his cheek with my hand and turned his
face back to mine. "He is no fool, is he? He will see
them. Do not show your face; it is still too pale and
clean. You should have used the dirt as I told you."
He kept a decent amount of space between us, one
I quickly eliminated. "Why are you being so polite?
You are propositioning me, remember? Act as if
you are."

"You will have to tell me how to do this," Salme
said, "for I have never seen a harlot, much less prop-
ositioned one."

"It is simple. You want me, and I want payment
for it." I swallowed as I saw one of the guards pause
and stare at us. "You may flatter me all you wish,
master," I said, loud enough for the guard to hear,
"but if you will make the shakab with me, you must
offer me more than pretty words."

"My words are only the beginning." He lifted his

hand and cupped my face. "I shall give you what-ever you ask, mistress."

He was better than I at making a pretense; I almost believed him. I took his hand and brought it down to cover my breast. "That is more like it."

The guard gave me a leering grin of approval and moved on.

Salme did not grab me, or fondle me. He kept his hand resting over my breast, exactly where I had placed it, as if touching me in so intimate a manner was nothing out of the ordinary.

My heart was pounding like the footsteps of a child in a hurry. "You do well for a man who has never seen or spoken to a harlot."

"My uncle raised me to respect women," he con-fided, his eyes twinkling as if it were all a game, instead of his life and mine. "He would beat me with a stick if he saw me doing thus."

"I could beat you with a stick now," I said, my voice low and furious as I saw the guards leaving the market. I pushed his hand away. "Have you and your companion heat madness, that you make assig-nations in the middle of the market? With guards looking for you and every other Semite fool enough to come into Riha?"

"We thought this quarter a safer place in which to hide." He grimaced. "The king sends search parties out each night. They go through the abandoned houses two and three times, so we can no longer hide in them."

"You have done no better to come to Meshnedef, for you cannot hide here," I said. "The king's men are everywhere here. A detachment of guards searched my house for you only last night."

"Why would they think we were at the home of a pretty woman?" he asked, suddenly concerned. "Did they disturb your family? They did not hurt you, did they?"

He seemed so sincere and upset that I almost forgave him for being a stupid man with no more brains than a small-headed goat.

"They made threats and stole some of our things, that is all. But that is not the point." I jabbed a finger into his chest. "You and your cousin should not be here in Riha. I told you to go, Salme. Why did you not listen to me?"

"Our work was not done. I begin to think you sent by Jehovah to watch over us," Salme said. "Do not worry. We are finished here, and only waiting a chance to leave the city unseen."

"That is what I am trying to tell you—you cannot leave now." I told him what Hlavat had told me about the inspections, searches, and the name voucher required for all who passed through the city gates. "Unless—can you obtain vouchers for you and Yofni?"

"Even if I knew how, there is no time. We must cross the river and inform our leaders and the assembly of what we have learned." He glanced back. "They are gone. I must find Yofni." He bent and brushed his mouth across my lips.

I touched my lips with my fingers. "Why did you do that?"

"Because there is no time to do more." He stroked his thumb over my cheek. "If only there was. You are Semite, just like us, are you not?"

"My mother was." I should not have told him that, but I was still astonished by the kiss. "She taught me the language of her people, and to believe in the One God." I saw his expression change. "What is it?"

"I knew it. I felt it, when I met you." He looked as if he might kiss me again.

"She is all I know of Semites," I told him. "I was born to a Rihan father, and I have lived here all my life."

"It matters not. I have so much I wish to tell you about our people." He sighed. "It must wait for another time. I must find somewhere safe for Yofni and me to hide until nightfall."

"Wait, I know of a place." I described Jela's house and how to find it. "No one will go near it, but I doubt the guards believe in bad luck, so do not stay there long."

"We will wait until the clouds cover the moon. You have to get out of Riha, so you may as well come with us. You can meet your people. Your mother likely has kin among us." He bent his head down so that our faces were close. "You must meet my uncle as well. He will think you brave for playing the harlot to protect me."

Play? Did he think it pretense? Of course he did; I had never told him differently. He thought me like other women, perhaps the daughter of a merchant, someone who should not be subjected to such language and touching. And yes, a part of me wished him to believe that, for I wanted him to admire and respect me. Almost as much as I wished him to touch me again.

That could not happen, so I told him the truth.

"It was not brave, and I did not have to pretend, Salme." I covered my head. "I *am* a harlot. I live and work in a house of harlots. The finest house in Meshnedef, in fact."

He did not grow angry, or look disgusted. He did not react much at all. He straightened and looked down at me. "I see."

"Do not feel upset. You said yourself that you have never been with a harlot, so how would you know that I was one?" Because I was beginning to sound like Ubalnu now, I moved past him. "May He be with you."

"Rahab." He came around me and stopped me. "You must leave Riha. Go before the full moon begins to wane. Go as far away from here as you can."

He was not asking me to leave the city with him and his cousin now, and that hurt more than telling him that I was a harlot. "Why?"

"I cannot say." He pressed his fingers to my lips. "Do not ask me. Just please, leave."

"Riha is my home," I told him. "I was born here. My mother's tomb is here. My father cast me out, but he remains here, in the merchants' quarter; my little sister as well. The only friends I have are harlots, and they live here, in Meshnedef with me. I have no one else. I cannot go."

He started to say something, and then Yofni was there, staring at me while he muttered something low to Salme.

"Remember the basket seller's house," I said. "Farewell."

Ubalnu complained about my tardy return the entire way home from the market, and continued to do so as she helped me unload the bundles of flax from the cart and carry them inside.

"You will have to do something very special for me in return for this," she grumbled as I placed the new linen thread skeins into a basket to take up to Tiamat's room. "You were there gossiping for so long that my nose sunburned. What is it about market that women love so much? Better to save your silver than to spend it on something that only makes more work for you. I shall never understand it."

"I am sorry." I turned and placed my hand on her shoulder. "I thank you for your patience. Banune has some salve that will cool your nose. Whatever favor you wish is yours." I kissed her cheek and left her gaping at me as I picked up the basket and climbed the stairs.

Tiamat was sitting before her vanity, slowly applying a new line of kohl around her eyes. The sight of the new linen thread chased some of the tiredness from her face.

"You should not have spent so much," she

scolded. "Oh, look at this blue-green. It is like sunlight on the sea." She lifted out one skein to admire the color.

"You told Akhete you had never seen the ocean."

"I do lie now and then, but only to men who do the same to me and their mothers and their wives, so the gods forgive me." She chuckled at herself as she sorted through the basket. "No red."

"For that, you must go to the temple of Moloch and petition the high priest. It is not worth the trouble." I set the basket by her loom. "I can warp it for you now, if you like."

"Banune worries I shall pine away from idleness." Tiamat slowly rose and came over to study her loom. "I think the dark green as a warp, perhaps twenty-four threads. Rahab, I am dying."

"Yes, the green is the ri—" I halted and stared at her. "What did you say? No. No, you are fine. You look more improved each day."

"The next fever spell is not far off, and when it comes, it will be my last." She put her arm around my shoulders. "Do not grieve for me. I have lived a long and mostly happy life. I shall go to the afterlife and be with my mother again."

I opened my mouth and closed it. I wanted to shout at her, but I could barely speak. "You are wrong. You are only tired."

"Death is not something to fear," she assured me. "We all die."

"We all live first. Many years, in your case." I began to pace around the room. "We will summon the healer. He will know something to prevent any more fever spells. We will keep you at rest. You need not work anymore. Every zanna in this house would be glad to care for you, as you have for us."

"I knew there was something special about you from the moment we met, when you were thinking of stealing my dates." She went to her bed. "Banune knows my wishes, and Hlavat has the scrolls to give to the magistrate. The others may be resentful at first, but they will come around. Remember that anger only invokes anger."

I stopped pacing. "Of what do you speak?"

"I have made you my heir, Rahab. Upon my death, you will become the mistress of the House of Palms." She said this as if it were no more than a gift of a wig.

"I do not want to be a harlot anymore," I told her, as harsh as I could make the words. "So I cannot be your heir. Find someone else."

"Before the guards took our weaving, I saw yours. I slipped into your room one night while you were working. It was what I thought it would be." She lay back on her bed and tugged the coverlet over herself. "A simple weave, and yet better than anything I have ever worked."

I did not want her praise. I wanted her to live. "Do you not hear me? I cannot be a harlot for the rest of my life. If you wish someone to be your heir, make it Banune or one of the others."

"You need not be a harlot; that is why I am telling you now. When I am gone, use the silver I leave you to buy more looms. Train the other zanna to work the wool and linen." She rubbed her eyes. "It will take time, and they will not like it at first, especially Ubalnu. Be persistent. Once you have enough rugs and cloth, you can begin to sell at the market."

"Harlots weaving." I made an exasperated sound. "Yes, it makes perfect sense."

"When you have earned enough to keep the household for two seasons," she said, "you may tell the men that they can seek their pleasures elsewhere."

I thought of Banune's spinning wheel, the enclosure for the sheep and goats, too large for what few animals we kept. Then there was Arwia's talent with blending dyes for cloth, and Karasbaal's skills at making garments. Even Zakiti, who displayed little talent for anything, was a keen bargainer. Were we to have a stall at market, I would have her manage it.

Then it came to me. "You were planning to do this all along."

"Eventually. I did not have enough saved yet to see us through two seasons, and when my fever spells grew worse I saw that we would need another skilled weaver to take my place." She held up her hands and gazed at them. "I knew it was you when I saw your fingers and palms. The threads mark us, do they not?"

"I shall not do it," I told her flatly. "You are not going to die."

"I expect you to keep our sisters together. Each has suffered enough in her life." Tiamat closed her eyes. "That is all I ask in return."

I would have argued further, but she was asleep.

*   *   *

"My lovely Rahab." Narath greeted me that night and took me into an affectionate embrace. He held me at arm's length to admire my robes. "I must speak with you. No," he added when I would have led him into one of the private rooms. "It is a fine night. Let us walk in the garden."

Outside the sky was clear and lit by the moon, a smile that widened each day. I knew Salme and Yofni would not be leaving Riha tonight, and wondered if they would get out at all. Patrols of guards had tripled over the last weeks, and with each new day more houses in the quarter were searched, and citizens suspected of treason were arrested and taken to the kele.

Tiamat's palms swayed gently over our heads. We had picked most of the dates from them, so only a few remained, and those she had instructed us to leave for the birds.

We must always give a little to those who have nothing, she had told Cook when the old woman had complained. *The gods smile on those who do.*

Was that why she had made me her heir? Because I had nothing? Why did it anger me so, to think of her plotting this all along? She had taken me from the street, provided for me, given me employment. She did not wish me to be a harlot forever, either. She was giving me everything I needed to achieve the life I could bear.

All I needed do was watch her die.

Narath stopped me, bringing my attention back to him. "You do not hear a word I say."

167

I flushed. "I am sorry. I was thinking of a friend. What did you have to tell me?"

"Things are changing for me, Rahab." He drew me down beside him on the stone bench. "I have done all I can do with rebuilding the walls. The king has cancelled shipments of building materials in order to buy more chariots and weapons. Everyone in Riha speaks of nothing but the invasion to come."

I pretended confusion to hide my dismay. "An invasion? By whom?"

"Semites." His mouth thinned. "Their tribes are massing just on the other side of the river. If they find a way to ford it and come into Canaan, they will only be a half day's ride from Riha. War is imminent."

"It is said that their god promised them the land of Canaan," I said carefully. "Perhaps they will not attack. They may only intend to settle here, in the hills, or out in the farm country to the east."

"My lovely one, you do not understand the politics or the territories involved. Riha has the only reliable source of water in the valley. They will need to take it before they march on the other cities." He rubbed his hand up and down the side of my arm in an absent gesture. "These Semites know the Sea People have been invading from the east. They know that Egypt, despite Pharaoh's promises, will take no action to stop them. They are as grasshoppers to us Canaanites, but they have the advantage of greater numbers. Such a swarm descending upon our land might choke the life out of it." He gripped my arm. "That is why you must come with me."

Now I truly was puzzled. "Come with you where?"

"To Hazor. They would not dare attack us there, not with the fortifications and the king's troops, all trained in Egypt. You will be safe there with me." He smiled. "I shall buy a little house for you, and visit you often."

"You ask me to come as your concubine."

"I do not like you making the shakab with other men," he admitted. "I would have you to myself. We will have to economize at first, but when I am made master builder of the city, I shall have enough to keep you and a small number of servants."

My heart was shattering. So much that I thought I could hear it. "Has your father found you a wife?"

"He has been speaking with—" he stopped and gave me a startled look. "How did you know?"

"A father is generally the one to arrange a marriage for a son. If you are to be the master builder of Hazor, you will need a wife of good social rank." I moved out of his grasp and stood. "A concubine, on the other hand, will only cause trouble in the family."

"No one need know about you." He rose and frowned down at me. "Do you not care for me, as I you? Have I been mistaken in your regard for me?"

I had been, evidently. "You care for me, Narath, but you will not marry me."

Now he looked a little angry. "Rahab, you are a harlot. I cannot marry a woman who has lain with other men. I must think of my family's honor. The children I shall father. No son of mine will have . . ." he trailed off.

"A whore for a mother. Of course, you are right." Everything inside me was dead, but I did not know why. I had never expected to marry Narath. I had never thought beyond the nights we had spent together. He was the only man who had never made me feel as if I were selling myself. Now he made me feel as if I had done far worse. "I am flattered by your offer, and I know it is a generous one. But I cannot go with you."

"You cannot stay here in Riha, not with the Semites poised to attack," he said. "It is too dangerous. You will be safer with me."

"I cannot, but I thank you for thinking of me." I pasted a smile on my face. "So, shall we go upstairs, then? Do you wish to spend a full night with me, or just an hour or two?"

"Do not speak to me like I am one of the others," he grated.

"But I am a harlot, Narath." I felt quite calm now. "That is how we speak. This is what I do."

"You need not be," he said, his voice growing louder. "Come with me to Hazor, and I shall give you a better life than this."

"A better life, but no marriage, and no children." I nodded. "You are right in thinking that. Who would wish to hold a feast and wonder how many of the men attending might have made the shakab with his wife?"

"If you were not a harlot, I would take you to

wife." He pulled me into his arms. "I cannot change what is."

"If I were not a harlot, you would never have met me." I wanted to hurt him then, wound him as he had me. "Even were I not, you would yet be polluting your future children. I have Semite blood."

He went still. "You, a Semite?"

"My mother was, and as such things are judged, so, too, am I." I said it plainly, with pleasure. "Her name was Jezere, and she was the daughter of a shepherd. My father met her in Maon, and she lied to him and told him that was the place of her birth. At the time, she was a servant in the house of her father's master."

His arms fell away from me. "You cannot be blamed for your mother's bad blood."

Let him know everything, so that it may choke him.

"She raised me in the Semite faith, to worship the One God," I continued. "I am as much a Semite as those tribes of grasshoppers massing at the river. So, Narath, do you still wish to take me to Hazor? Can you risk having a Semite as a concubine? It would be a dangerous thing. What would you tell your king if I turned traitor?"

I did not hear his reply. He slapped me, so hard that it threw me to the ground. When I rose on my hands and knees, and spit out the blood in my mouth, he was gone.

"Yes," I whispered, knowing I would never see him again. "I loved you, too."

CHAPTER

12

Narath did not return to the House of Palms. No one spoke of him, but as the days passed and he did not come to spend a night with me, the other zanna became aware of my loss. No one asked any questions, but I noticed that each woman treated me in a gentle fashion, bringing me food and drink or taking on one of my chores.

Although I had been the one to drive him away, I missed him terribly. It seemed all I could do to rise in the morning and go on through the day. I thought over our last conversation in the garden until I could repeat every word we had said to each other. After my anger faded, at times I even thought myself foolish for driving him away. My life would have been better with him in Hazor, something I felt even more keenly at night, when I had to smile and pretend with any man who offered for me.

It was Banune who put an end to my sulking. "There will be plenty of rain tonight," she said over our morning meal. We had fallen into the custom of rising before Cook and the other zanna, and preparing our own meal, so we were alone at the table. "The leg I once broke has been aching since midnight."

I broke the lehem I was supposed to be eating into small pieces and let the crumbs fall atop the porridge I could not swallow. "As you say."

"You can carry one of the flax bundles up to the roof this afternoon, when the sun drops low," she informed me, "and spread them out so that the stems may soak."

"Tiamat has plenty of linen thread." I had slept little and wanted to go back to bed. Sleeping kept me from thinking. "I do not feel like hauling all of that flax upstairs."

"I do not care what you feel," Banune said. "I am spinning the flax; you can carry it up to the roof."

"Ask Zakiti. She grows fat; she can use the work." I tossed my untouched meal into the slops bucket for the goats and glared at her. "I do enough."

Banune folded her arms. "I do not see that you should be spared work after losing one of our best regulars."

"He was *my* regular, and I did not lose him." I was rigid with indignation. "*He* left *me*."

"Men do not leave us. They tire of us. They get married or find a new woman or run out of money. If you did not know that before, you know it now." There was not a single glimmer of pity in her eyes, and she barred my path to the door when I tried to leave the kitchen. "No, Rahab. You will not go up-stairs and sleep through the day again. Come, Lazy One." She picked up the slops bucket. "You can feed the animals with me now."

"I am not lazy. I do the work of two women," I told her.

"You did the work of two women once. Of late all you are good for is frowning, wasting food, and snoring." She handed me the slops bucket. "Either you feed the animals with me or empty the privy pots by yourself."

I trudged out to the enclosure and opened the gate. The goats and sheep were separated by a fence that ran down the middle of the enclosure. As I went to fill the trenchers for the goats on one side, Banune put out grain and hay for the sheep.

One of the goats, the old, bad-tempered male, tried to prod me aside with his long horns and nearly overturned the trencher. I turned to face him.

"I very much like stew with goat meat," I told him. "And we get no milk out of you." I bent down to right the trencher and saw dirt disappearing into a hole in the ground behind it. "Banune, what is this hole here?"

She glanced over. "Tia thinks it was once a well in the old city. We fill in the hole but the winter rains keep washing the dirt away."

I bent down and looked. The hole did not seem wide enough for a well; it did not drop down straight, but seemed to angle off to someplace under the enclosure gate. I looked around the yard, which had scanty soil and much gravel. Then I saw a fragment of white in the dirt near the edge of the hole and picked it up. It was a piece of a curved seashell.

The billy goat bleated at me, so I finished pouring out his meal. Banune came over to look at the hole.

"It does not look like a well," I told her. "Too narrow and not straight enough. I think it might belong to the Shell People." I handed her the bit of shell.

She made a face. "A tomb hole."

The Shell People were the first to build Riha, so long ago that their true name and language were lost to us. All we really knew of them was that they buried the bodies of the dead in strange pits in the ground—but without the heads. The heads they kept in their dwellings. Robur had once shown me and Tezi the skull of one of their dead, found by a slave who uncovered one of their houses under ours while digging in the garden. The skull had been covered with a curious plaster and possessed realistic-looking "eyes" made of curled seashells.

"We can fill it in later." I watched as the female goat herded her two kids over to the second trencher, where they all ate together. The kids were forever jostling and butting for a bigger share of the slops. I thought of Tezi, and how she would laugh at their antics. I ached to see my little sister, for my one visit had not been nearly long enough, but I did not want to return to the merchants' quarter. I did not fear seeing my father as much as I feared what I might say if I did.

"She is pregnant again," Banune said after running her hand along the nanny goat's side. "Another pair of mouths to feed before summer arrives."

It seemed ridiculous to speak of goats and kids. "Maybe you should give her some linens to use."

"I am more likely to stuff several in your mouth." Banune eyed me.

"I have not complained." Indeed, I had been very silent since Narath had stopped coming to the house. I took pride in suffering in silence.

"One does not have to speak to complain." She took the slops bucket from me. "I expected Tiamat to make me serve her heir. Perhaps if you leave us, she will choose someone more worthy of being mistress of this house."

I stared at her. "I do not wish to be a harlot, or her heir. The thought of it makes me want to vomit."

"That makes two of us. Oh, Tia asked me if I would serve you as I have her. At the time I said yes, but I think I shall have to change my mind." She shrugged. "I have no desire to serve someone who permits a man's stupidity to turn her into a shrew. Why, I would rather serve Ubalnu as my mistress. Gods know, she is a shrew, but at least she is an amusing one."

"Why would you serve, when you can leave?" I countered.

"I cannot leave, Rahab. Tiamat owns me. She bought me from the same slave caravan from which she obtained Ubalnu and Karasbaal." She opened the gate and went out of the enclosure.

"Ubalnu and Karasbaal said Tia freed you," I said, following her back into the kitchen.

"She freed them. My servitude cannot be rescinded." She put the bucket back in its place. "I am a life slave."

I had never heard of such a thing. "How is that possible?"

"My birth killed my mother, who was my father's favorite house slave," she said. "It was the law in our village. An eye for an eye, a life for a life. Usually such a child is killed and buried with the mother. I am fortunate that my greedy father convinced the elders to make my sentence slavery for life, so that he could sell me and recoup some of his loss."

"Tia could free you and no one would ever know," I said.

She shook her head. "My slave voucher states very plainly the condition of my slavery. It is valid under the code of Canaanite law. I was branded with the mark of a life slave as well, so even if the voucher were destroyed, anyone who sees the mark will know. I can never own property, marry, or bear free children. For life." She smiled at me. "Now, tell me again how wretched your situation is. How terrible it is to be free to do as you wish. To tell a man who would have adored you and supported you that it was not good enough."

I felt miserable, as she intended me to. "You should have told me."

"I do not show my grief, Rahab. It is personal, and

mine to suffer." Her expression softened. "I am sorry about Narath. He was a pleasant, kind man."

My eyes burned. "He was."

"He was also proud and self-interested, a man who has walled himself in as much as he has Riha." She sighed. "I do not think that he is the only man in the world who will ever care for you."

I would not weep. Not in front of a woman who had suffered, and would always suffer, more than I could bear. "I pray you are right."

She gave me a brisk nod. "Let us go and wake up Karasbaal. He sleeps as much as you have these days, and it is his turn to empty those privy pots."

Things were a little better after Banune talked me out of my poor spirits. I stopped sleeping through my sadness, and tried to work instead. I found pleasure at the loom again, and my weave grew a foot each day. Even the nights were not so bad, considering that I spent them serving men for whom I cared nothing. The only thing that truly plagued me was my hair, which combined with the rising temperatures, made wearing wigs uncomfortable.

"It must have been beautiful," Tiamat said to me when I took off the dark brown wig I put on before the guests began to arrive and showed her my problem. "Praise the goddess of beauty, it grows like fire burns. I think there is almost an inch and a half now."

"I should shave it all off." I looked at my reflection. To my eyes, I looked like an overgrown infant. "I am used to the wigs now."

"No, let it grow back." Tia ran a hand over my new growth of hair. "We can make the pads in your wigs lighter, which will help with the sweating and discomfort."

Someone knocked at the door and called for me.

"I wager Darbas is here." I sighed and placed the wig back on my head. "Since Narath has not returned, he has been vowing to take his place."

"That must be to impress the other men," Tia said, her eyes dancing with mirth, "for if he buys an entire night with you, the most he can do is sleep through it."

Zakiti was waiting outside, panting and red-faced from hurrying up from the first floor. "Man," she wheezed out. "Downstairs. Asking for you."

I glanced at the window, and saw that the sun had barely set. Zakiti was too breathless to say more, so I took her arm and helped her to her room before going down to see who had arrived this early.

"He would not come inside," Banune said. She was carrying two wine skins into the great room. "He waits for you in the garden."

I walked out through the kitchen to see a familiar figure standing beneath the palms. "Father?"

Robur looked over at me. "It took me three days to find you."

"Why would you look?" I thought of my sister. "Is it Tezi? Is she ill?"

"No, your sister is well. Not very happy, but she is no longer alone." He lifted his chin. "I got rid of the slave and hired an old couple to watch after her." He glanced at the top of my head. "What have you done to your hair?"

"I have no hair, thanks to your wife," I said, touching the dark curls by my cheek. "It is a wig."

He nodded, swallowed, and regarded his sandals intently. "Helsbah has left me. She lives in the house of her brother, the minister of temples. She has petitioned the king for a divorce, so in a few months, she will no longer be my wife."

"I cannot say I am sorry to hear it."

"Before she left, she told me that you had never struck her, or practiced magic on her." He gave me a miserable look. "She said it was a trick, to get rid of you. She hated you. She laughed and said she was glad you were dead."

I lifted my brows. "I hope you corrected her."

"I did not tell her of your visit to me, or that you are . . ." he could not bring himself to say it. "Why did you not tell me that she lied?"

I remembered what I had said to him, the day he had cast me out. *You condemn me, your own daughter, on her lies?* "I did tell you. You chose to believe her over me."

"You should have tried harder," he shouted. "You should have made me see what she was."

"Still you blame me." If it had not been so pathetic, I might have laughed. "Have you anything else to say? I have work to do."

"I cannot bring you back under my roof. The boset would be unbearable. People will think you . . . what is done is done." He fumbled at his belt and took out a purse. "Here. I shall bring more to you when I have it."

I stared at the purse. I had quickly learned how to size up their contents with a glance. From the way it bulged, he had brought me at least two or three mina. A payment of conscience, to relieve him of his guilt.

"I cannot take it." I turned and walked back to the kitchen.

Robur caught up with me before I went inside. "It is silver, honestly earned. Take it."

"There is only one way I earn silver, Father," I said, "and that I cannot do with you. Keep it. Use it to provide for my sister."

"Rahab." His anguish was plain now. "What would you have me do, then?"

"Forget me."

I left him outside, knowing he would never cross the threshold, knowing he would walk home feeling the weight of his guilt with each step. I wanted to rejoice, for it was the sort of revenge I had only dreamed of, but I could not. I could only think of Tezi, and how lonely she would be, growing up alone with only an old pair of servants and an embittered father to care for her.

She might be as lonely as me.

Darbas did not fulfill his vow to spend the night with me—again—and there were fewer men than usual, thanks to the guard patrols.

"They stop anyone they please and search them," the local cobbler said as Arwia held his feet on her lap and rubbed them. "As if I am hiding Semites under my cloak."

Akhete had come, sober for once, and joked about the guards' ability to find anything. "The king must be drafting blind men, for they cannot see that which is in front of their faces. Even when it is as big as a statue of Moloch."

Darbas laughed. "The red drapings would not tip them off?"

"You heard of the latest farce, haven't you?" The oil merchant chuckled. "Two spies have been hiding in an empty hovel, only a few streets from here, a week or more. The merchants living around the house finally sent a messenger to the guard, begging them to come and evict the Semites before they burned down the neighborhood."

He had to be speaking of Salme and Yofni.

"Did they catch the spies?" I asked as casually as I could.

"No, for when the fools finally broke the door down, the house was empty." Akhete held out his goblet for Banune to fill. "All the spies had left behind was their cloaks and a bit of food."

"They will turn Meshnedef upside down, looking for them," Darbas predicated in a gloomy tone. He patted my hip. "Let us go enjoy the night while we can, Rahab."

I remembered Banune's words and made myself grateful that the trader was very quick. It took only half an hour to see to him upstairs and escort him out. I did not even object to the fact that he shorted me on silver and spilled wine on my robe. All I could think of was Salme and Yofni, and how long they would last trying to evade the guard.

After I showed Darbas out, I considered retiring for the night. The other zanna could take care of the men waiting, and I did not think I was capable of keeping up a pretense of happiness and interest. I was on my way to tell Banune, when I heard a soft knocking.

More men.

With effort, I straightened my shoulders and went to greet them. There were two, both dressed in shabby robes and the turbans of desert traders, which were draped to cover the nose and mouth. Both looked as if they had just come in from a long journey.

I controlled my frown, but only just. "Welcome to the House of Palms," I said as I opened the door for them. "I am—"

"Rahab," the taller one said, and I knew from the voice that it was Salme. "Yofni and I need your help."

I pulled them inside and shut the door quickly. "Are there guards following you? Were you seen coming here?"

"We do not think so," Yofni told me. "We need rooms."

"This is not an inn." I could not believe they had come here. "Try the Gilded Thorn at the corner of the next street. They do not look too closely at those who take a room."

Salme shook his head. "We do not dare; there are guards posted outside every inn and caravan house in the quarter. We need only one room."

One room for two spies in a quarter where guards were searching for them this very moment. The day I had saved Evora and her daughters came back to me, as well as Tiamat's warning.

. . . before you interfere with another person's life, you must have the means to help them.

Salme had never told me he and his cousin were spies, but there was no other reason for them to be so long in Riha. To offer them aid was to risk the life of every woman in the house. "I cannot do it. I cannot hide you here. You must go."

"It is only until we can find a way over the wall," Yofni said. "Then we will bother you no more."

"You cannot climb over the wall," I told him. "It is patrolled, just as the streets are."

Banune looked out at us. "Rahab? Do you need me?"

"No, Banune, all is well." I lowered my voice and spoke to Salme. "If someone saw you—if you are discovered in our house—"

"I know." He took my cold hand in his. "I would not put this burden on you, but there was no one else. We did not dare try to leave the quarter."

I could not help them. It was too much to ask. The guards could come at any moment to search the house.

"Do not fear, Rahab," Salme said quietly. "For He is always with us."

"He is not here now, or He would whisk you out of here and over the wall." I needed time to think. "You cannot go in where the other men are. They will wish to speak with you, and you will give yourselves away." I led them into a private room. "You can stay here and rest for an hour, but that is all."

Yofni, who was ashen-faced and sweating, sat down heavily and held his head in his hands.

"Is he ill?" I asked Salme.

"We have not eaten or slept for two days," Salme told me. "Can you spare some food for us?"

"Yes." That much I could do for them. "Stay here."

CHAPTER
13

I retrieved some lehem, cheese, and fruit from the kitchen, as well as a water jug. When I walked back to the private room, Banune intercepted me.

"Akhete has taken an interest in Ubalnu, and Zakiti has the cobbler upstairs." She glanced down at the amount of food I carried. "You have two in the private room?"

"A pair of traders, just in from the desert." I tried to think of an excuse to keep her out of the room. "They are shy ones."

"Oh." Banune never liked timid men, as she tended to overwhelm them. "Have them wait for Ubalnu to become available, then. I dare say she and Akhete will not suit each other for long. They are too much alike."

"I shall take them."

"Both?" Her eyebrows rose. "That is not like you."

"I am feeling restless after Darbas." I tried to

186

sound as if I was. "It will keep me from thinking about Narath."

"Very well, I shall tidy up. If you change your mind, send one of them to Ubalnu." She went back into the great room.

I hurried back to Salme and Yofni, and watched them devour the food like starving beggars. They were no better off than the miskin, either, not when they were fugitives with no means to leave the city and rejoin their people. I tried to think of where they could go from here, but nothing came to mind. People were frightened; strangers were noticed and reported. I could not even trust the other zanna to keep silent.

"Is there some room in the house that is not used?" Salme asked me. "We desperately need to rest and sleep a few hours."

"The only place in the house where the other women do not go freely are our bedchambers on the third floor," I told him. "We each have our own. But the doors do not bolt, and there is no guarantee someone will not come in and find you in mine."

"A gardening shed outside will do just as well," Yofni suggested.

"We have an open-sided lean-to for the animals, and a garden, but neither would hide you from sight." I gnawed at my lower lip. What was I thinking? I could not hide two men in my room. "Are you certain that you have no friends in the city? No one sympathetic to you?"

Salme smiled sadly. "Only you, Rahab."

Ubalnu came in without warning and inspected the two Semite spies. "Hoarding all the interesting ones tonight, Rahab?"

"Not deliberately." I went to Salme and sat on his lap, curling my arm around his neck and leaning close. "She likes to be aggressive," I murmured against his ear. "Show no interest in her." I chuckled as if confiding something amusing to him.

He nodded slightly.

Ubalnu considered Yofni, dismissed him with a sniff, and sauntered over to Salme. She ran her fingernail down the side of his jaw, not quite hard enough to leave a mark. "For a sand rat, you are a handsome one. Do you like to beg for your tiph'eret?"

"I have never had to," Salme told her, his voice dry.

Banune looked in the room. "Ubalnu, Akhete grows impatient, and he does not want me."

I played with a fold of Salme's turban, watching the other zanna out of the corner of my eyes. I could tell from her expression that she was wavering between staying here and returning to the oil merchant.

"You do not charge much, do you?" Yofni asked in an anxious fashion. "My cousin and I are not rich men."

"Then I am too expensive for you." Visibly disgusted, Ubalnu walked out and slammed the door behind her.

Relief made me sag against Salme for a moment

before I climbed off his lap. "The two of you must leave. Complain about the price being too high as you go."

"Rahab—"

I held up my hand. "Go to the side of the house and wait in the garden, by the palms. I shall come to you after the others are asleep. It is the only way I may get you to the third floor without them seeing you."

When I would have opened the door, Salme put a hand out to stop me. "How will you conceal us from the other women? You said you cannot bolt the door."

"I shall stay with you while you sleep tonight." I had few furnishings, and no chest large enough to hold one of them, let alone both. "I have a loom in one corner of my room; you can sleep behind that. No one who comes in will see you."

"What if the city guard comes to search the house?" Yofni demanded. "They will tear apart your loom to get to us."

He was right; the loom wouldn't stop the guards, and if they were found in the house, all our heads would adorn pikes in short order. "I shall think of something," I promised. "Now go, and remember to be scathing about paying my price."

I walked them out, making a show of sighing as they complained about the high cost of pleasure. Banune heard them and came out to discover what had happened.

"Desert traders, always so cheap. That is why so

many of them end up wealthy; they cannot bear to part with a beqa." Banune patted my shoulder. "Do not let it worry you."

"I shall not." I smiled at her. "Do you need me to help with the cleaning?"

"No, it is all done." She yawned. "Would you check on Tia before you go to sleep? I have not been to see her since the evening meal, and she may want something."

"I shall be happy to." I was already planning to go up to Tiamat's room. Before I brought Salme and Yofni back into the house, I had to tell her.

Tiamat was seated before her loom when I went upstairs to speak with her, and smiled over her shoulder at me without stopping her work.

"This pattern intoxicates me," she said as I came to stand beside her. "Hours pass unnoticed, and I can only seem to stop when I am too tired to lift my arms."

"It is wonderful." And it was, with a color pattern that shifted and moved across the cloth as though it were alive. "Such fine thread, too. I shall have to set aside my wool and try the linen."

"You might blend them, although wool embraces another type of fiber much better than flax. Flax is stubborn." She finished her final row and looped her warp thread to the right post. "I think that is enough for tonight." She rose and stretched. "Did Banune send you? She makes herself my mother these days."

She looked almost like her old self, busy, vibrant, and content. I thought of leaving Salme and Yofni in the garden and bolting our doors. "Tia, I must tell you something. It is what I told Narath, that drove him away from me."

She glanced at me. "I know you are a Semite, Rahab. I have always known."

My jaw dropped for a moment. "But I lied to you. I told you I was not, the day I came here."

"You are not a very good liar." She patted my cheek. "Banune knows as well. She passed your room while you were praying to your One God. Some of the slaves in her former master's house were Semites, so she recognized the language. She will say nothing."

"You said nothing, all this time."

"People believe in many gods." She shrugged. "Given how Semites are treated in Riha, I was more concerned with keeping it a secret."

"That is why I must speak with you." I came and led her to a chair, and sat on the floor before her. "I went to see my sister and my father some time ago, and when I was returning to Meshnedef, I met two strangers."

I told her everything: how I had discovered Salme was a Semite from the first words he had said to me; Yofni drawing the dagger; how I had advised them to disguise their faces and leave Riha before they were arrested. I told her of my second encounter with Salme at the market, when I had made a pretense to keep him from being arrested, and directed him and his cousin to hide in Evora and Jela's abandoned house.

"From what Akhete said, they were betrayed by Jela's neighbors, and had to flee the house," I said. "Then . . . it is my fault, you see. When I was with Salme at the market, I told him that I truly was a harlot, and lived in a house of harlots. There are not so many in Meshnedef that he had trouble finding me."

"He and his cousin are here now," Tiamat said. I nodded. "They wish you to give them sanctuary."

"I gave them some food and drink, and sent them outside, into the garden." I gazed up at her. "I come to beg your permission to give them sanctuary."

Tiamat rose and went to the window. She stood there for a long time, her hands resting on the edge, her eyes looking not down into the garden, but at her two beloved palms.

"The khamsin will come soon," she said idly. "The trees always know. They must feel the change in the air, or taste it in the water. I think at first they must hate it, because they cannot hide or flee. Then they remember their strength; that they may never run from the storm. That is what makes a tree stand against the khamsin. Because it accepts that it can do nothing else."

"I know what it is that I ask of you," I said. "It is much more dangerous than it was with Evora and the children. If you say no, I shall send them away."

"I would like to tell you to do that," she said, her tone cool. "These men are what I have most feared."

Did she despise Semites, as Narath did? Had I made another terrible mistake, confiding in her? "They only wish to leave the city."

"They are the storm that will tear you away from us." She turned to me. "I shall permit you to hide them here, but this time, I want something in exchange."

"Anything."

"Sanctuary for sanctuary." Her eyes had a frightening glitter. "Whatever comes of this, whatever these men bring to Riha, you will stay here, in the House of Palms. Tell them they must save this house and our sisters."

"They will not harm us—"

"They will not have to. I have spoken to Hlavat and some of the other men. There is an army waiting on the other side of the river. An army of Semite nomads and their allies, the hapiru. These people can live wherever they pitch their tents, and worship their one god." She went to her loom and threaded her fingers through the warp. "They will not come to the city gates and beg entrance. They will not petition the king at the temple of Moloch. To them Riha is not a prize; it is an obscenity, and an obstacle. Can you blame them for wishing to destroy us?"

"Riha is well guarded and fortified." The hair on my arms prickled and I could not stop shivering. "They may not succeed."

"Pharaoh, with all his might and his armies, could not keep the Semites building his pyramids for him in Egypt. I rather doubt Khormad has a flea's chance against their wrath." Tiamat leaned her head against the loom post. "It is a kind of justice, when you think about it. How many children have died to feed Riha's gods? This city has become an evil place, soaked in the blood of innocents."

"It is not our fault."

"We permitted it. We blinded ourselves to it. Now the Semites will come, like the khamsin." Tiamat's face looked drawn and old now. "No matter. You have power and influence over these men. Use it to stay here and keep the house and our sisters safe."

"If I can," I said slowly, "I shall do so. I swear to you."

She nodded. "Tomorrow night, bring them here. My window is closest to the wall. Once the patrol passes, they can climb across on ropes and lower themselves over the side."

I waited until I was sure the other zanna were asleep before I crept downstairs and made my way out to the garden.

Outside I saw no sign of Salme and Yofni, and fear gripped me.

Jehovah, no. They could not have been caught. We would have heard the shouts of the guards. I looked up toward Tiamat's window and saw her watching. That was when I saw the two shadows moving down the trunks of the palms.

Salme jumped the last foot to the ground and went to help Yofni. Both held short lengths of cord in their hands and had shed their sandals, to better grip the trunks.

"Patrols?" I asked Salme, who nodded. "Come inside, quickly. Make no sound."

I led them in through the kitchen and there waited, listening for movement in the house before we proceeded up the stairs. I was at the front, and paused every few steps to check for any noise. Once we were on the third floor, I guided them to my room and closed the door.

Salme pulled the shade down over the window while Yofni sat down by the wall and rested. I took what extra blankets I had from my chest and spread them on the floor. My own sleeping mat I moved by the door, where I would have to sleep until we were able to get them out of the house. I went to the window, where Salme was looking through a crack in the shade.

"No sign of the guards," he told me, his voice low.

"They have gone back to their barracks to sleep," I said. "You should rest while you can."

He nodded. "So should you."

Yofni moved my mat back to its place and took a blanket and a sitting position by the door.

"I shall take the door, mistress. I do not sleep hard, or startle easily," he said. "Anyone who tries to come in will wake me first."

There was nothing else for me to do but try to sleep myself, so I lay down on my mat. Only a foot or so away from me, Salme did the same. I was not used to having anyone in this room with me, or being so close to a man and yet not touching him.

A moment later I heard steady breathing and glanced over to see Yofni dozing while sitting up.

"I could not sleep like that," I said to Salme. "How does he do it?"

"Too many years guarding camps in the wilderness." Salme pillowed his head with his arm. "Why did you change your mind about letting us stay here?"

"I am demented," I said. "Probably." I could not tell him about Tiamat; he would not understand, and it might even alarm him to know their presence was not only my secret. "Why have Semites come into Canaan? Is it to fulfill Jehovah's promise, as my mother told me?"

"It began when we came out of the wilderness. Jehovah directed Moses to appoint his brother Aaron's son, Eleazar, as the new high priest of Israel. Moses then placed his hands on Joshua and named him as his successor. I was there the day it happened." Salme grimaced. "It was a frightening day. Moses led our fathers and grandfathers out of Egypt, and Jehovah spoke to him. He is almost like a god himself."

"But Joshua is not," I guessed.

"Joshua is an inspiring leader, but he is different. He came to us after Moses died, and told us what Jehovah commanded." His gaze grew faraway. "I shall remember his words all the days of my life.

That we would come together, all the people, and go over the Jordan. That Jehovah had given to us every place that we would walk, from the wilderness and Lebanon as far as the Euphrates, and all the land of the Hittites, and out to the Great Western Sea. Joshua told us that no man would be able to stand before our army, as He would be with us, wherever we go."

Salme told me how since Moses's death Joshua had followed Jehovah's will, and had sent out officers from his army for months to locate all the tribes scattered throughout the wilderness. The officers, who acted as messengers, had spoken of Moses's will and Joshua's vow to bring the Semites into the Promised Land.

"The tribes have been gathering on the east side of the Jordan for more moons than I can count," he said. "Other officers have been to cities all over northern Canaan to scout defenses and learn who and what might challenge our army."

"Joshua is a persuasive man." I was hot, and without thinking I pulled off my wig.

Salme smiled. "For a man of few words, he is. He never speaks to us as Moses did." His gaze shifted. "What happened to your hair?"

I put my hand up to touch the damp, short hair covering my scalp now. "My stepmother cut it off the day I was cast out of my family." I told him how it had happened, and what she had told Robur before leaving him. "I can never go home, but at least my father knows the truth."

"You have had a hard time of it."

"Everyone does in some way or another." I did not want his pity, or to dwell on what could not be changed. "I have only heard of Moses in my mother's stories," I said. "What is he like?"

"He was not as tall as me, but he seemed to tower over every other man, as ancient and immovable as the mountains." He moved his hand in a sweeping gesture. "You felt you were in the presence of Jehovah whenever you were near Moses; the power of our God enveloped him."

The thought of such a man intimidated me. "Moses died recently?"

"Just before Yofni and I were sent to Jericho." Salme's expression turned sad. "Many of our people were in despair, but Joshua seemed to know that it was his time. He took command as if born to it."

"What is Joshua like?"

"He is a soldier." Salme rolled over onto his back. "A powerful man, but not an easy one. He does not permit his men to question orders, and disciplines those who try. He is not one for praise, either." Salme's voice turned wry. "I was successful in bringing back one of the mountain tribes that had held out against the summons to arms. It was dangerous; they were resistant at first, and for a time I thought they might kill me rather than join us. When I rode into camp with them, Joshua said nothing to me, not a single word of praise or thanks."

"Perhaps he was busy." I disliked this Joshua already.

"Not too busy to make me captain of the army the

next day." He put an arm over his eyes. "Then I was given the order to come into Riha. That is how he rewards, with a promotion and a more dangerous task."

"Yet you risk your life for him."

"Joshua commands respect and loyalty. In that, he is very much like Moses." He sighed. "I hope it serves him in the time ahead."

I thought of what Tiamat had said. "He is coming to destroy Riha, is he not? That is why he sent you here. To see how it could be done."

Salme did not speak for so long I thought he had fallen asleep. Then he said, "Rahab, this is the land Jehovah promised us. We knew when we came out of the wilderness that we would have to fight for it. But it is ours."

I wanted to believe him, but part of me could not put faith in a claim that could never be proven. "How can you be so certain?"

"We have earned it." He turned to face me. "You do not know what it was like, to live in the wilderness. There was never enough food, and we always had to be on our guard. Semites are not only despised in Riha, you see. We lost so many to sickness and injury, and then there were always attacks by raiders and slavers. One tribe disappeared altogether; we could find no trace of them and fear they may have been massacred. It could have happened to any of us. We wandered like lost children, never knowing what lay ahead, or what followed behind."

"You could have gone back to Egypt," I pointed out. "There was work there."

"Work, yes. Slave labor building the pyramids, the foundations of which are already soaked with our blood." His voice turned bitter. "My father's grandfather was a stonecutter. He was fitting a casing stone on an upper level when he fell. The Egyptian overseers left his broken body on the sand and whipped anyone who tried to go near it. The work allotted for that day had to be finished before anyone could help him. It is said that he died in great agony, staring up into the sun and calling for his family."

I regretted reminding him of it. "I am sorry."

"There is no need." He reached across the space between us, and took my hand in his. "The long, cruel years of slavery and wandering are over. We are home, Rahab, and He is always with us."

CHAPTER
14

Somehow we slept that night, although none of us well. The slightest sound woke me to find Salme at the window and Yofni listening at the door. It seemed forever until the first rays of the sun lightened the darkness.

When it was time for me to go downstairs, I had them hide in the small space behind my loom and cover themselves with the long length of weave I had already completed.

"I know it is uncomfortable," I told them as I put away the extra blankets that might also betray their presence, "but if someone should walk in, you will not be seen. I shall bring you food as soon as I am able to."

I had to then go downstairs and act as if nothing had happened. Banune was there before me, feeding the coals in the cooking pit to warm the dough for the morning's baking. I greeted her and went to milk the goats, and then returned to share a simple meal of fruit and cheese with her.

"A pity those two caravaneers did not stay last night." Banune topped a piece of lehem with cheese and sliced onion. "If I should see them again, I could persuade them return."

I nearly choked on my grapes. "They were dirty," I said, knowing how she disliked unclean men. "I would not have them back here."

She nodded, satisfied with my opinion. "How was Tia last night?"

"Happily weaving at her loom." My appetite was gone, but I tried to force down a little more. "Do you think it will rain tonight?"

"The sky is filled with clouds; likely it will before sunset." She glanced at me. "You were not planning to go anywhere today, I hope."

"I thought to take the rest of the flax up to the roof, as this could be the last of the rain until winter," I explained. "I have no plans to go anywhere, but why should I not?"

"Lukur is dedicating the new temple of Moloch at midday today. There have been heralds all through the streets, calling out the general invitation to the people." Banune frowned. "Haven't you heard them?"

If I had, I had paid no attention to it. "Oh, yes, I forgot about that."

"Whenever they dedicate a new temple, people like to drink and behave like fools," she warned me. "The miskin are not permitted in the citadel, so they will have their revelries here. The streets will become crowded and dangerous. It is best to stay inside until it is all over."

Tiamat and I had to get the men out of here tonight. "How long will this take?"

"Two days, perhaps three." She shrugged. "However long the casks of wine sent out by the king last."

Karasbaal came into the kitchen. He was dressed in one of his finest robes, and had ironed his hair so that it fell long and flat to his shoulders. For once his face was bare of cosmetics.

"You are up early," Banune said as she finished her meal and prepared a bowl with fruit and lehem as she did every morning now for Tiamat. "Rahab, watch the dough does not rise too much. I shall be back in a moment."

Karasbaal sat down beside me and reached for a pomegranate. Without preamble, he asked me, "You were the daughter of the rug seller in the king's marketplace, were you not?"

"I was." Tiamat was the only one in the house who knew my father's name, and she would never have mentioned it to Karasbaal. "Who told you this?"

"His wife has hired me to go to the temple dedication with her," he said, cutting the fruit into thick slices. "Your mother uses me often, for many things. She has become one of my best patronesses."

"My mother is dead. That woman was my stepmother." Feeling sick, I rose to my feet. "I wish you joy of her."

"You also have a younger sister, do you not? One who has not yet had her moon time?"

I froze and stared down at him. "What about her?"

"Your father's wife also makes use of her."

I grabbed him up by the front of his robe and had him against the nearest wall before he could speak. "Did you touch her? Did she give her to you?"

He showed me his teeth, stained red with pomegranate juice. "I do not make the shakab with children."

I shook him. "How does she use her?"

"She has not. Not yet. Today she will, Rahab." He looked down at my hands. "She will use your sister to gain favor with the high priest."

"How?" I nearly shouted.

"Lukur needs sacrifices, and everyone knows children make the best sort," he said calmly. "Today she will take your sister to the dedication, and give her to the god Moloch."

"No." Disgusted, I released him. "My father would not allow it. You are lying."

"Your father spends his day at the shop, your stepmother said." Karasbaal straightened his fine robe. "The old couple will not be able to stop her from taking the child. By the time your father comes home, they will already be at the temple."

I braced myself against the table with one hand. "She would not dare. He will kill her."

"For giving Lukur a child in sacrifice?" He shook his head. "She will be honored, and protected."

"Not today." I shoved past him, but he caught my arm. "Let go of me, Karasbaal."

"She will reach your sister before you can," he said. "But I can save her for you, Rahab. I am to meet them at the temple of Moloch. I can take the girl from Helsbah and bring her to you. She will be safe—if you meet my price."

"I shall give you all I have. Seven mina of silver," I told him. "If that is not enough, I shall borrow more."

"I do not want your silver." He leaned so close I could see every pore, every blemish on his skin. "I want you."

The thought of Tezi drove everything else from my head. "Fine, you can have me."

"Whenever I choose. However I choose." He ran the tip of his finger in a line down between my breasts.

His touch made me feel nothing but disgust and pity. That he should want me so much and use my sister's life to get his desire simply made him more pathetic than ever. "As you say."

"So eager now. You had better be the same when I summon you to my room." He bent down and pressed his mouth over mine for a moment. "You will have to show more enthusiasm than that."

"You bring my sister to me, alive and unharmed, first. Then you can have me, and my enthusiasm, ten times a night."

"Oh, but I cannot get her out of the citadel alone," he said. "You will have to come with me."

*   *   *

Karasbaal gave me only a few minutes to dress and prepare myself before we were to leave.

"Wear your yellow robes—I like those—and paint your face," he ordered me. "Rub some scented oil into your skin; you smell like milk." He eyed my head. "Get rid of that wig; it is ugly. Wear the expensive red one that Tiamat gave you."

"Red is the banned color," I reminded him.

"Hardly anyone in Riha has red hair," he told me. "You will stand out in the crowd. And Rahab." He tapped my cheek with his hand. "Do not think of cheating me, or I shall take my price out of your sister."

I hurried upstairs to change, forgetting about Salme and Yofni in my haste. In my room, I tore off my wig and garments. A polite cough reminded me that I was not alone.

"I am leaving for the citadel," I told them as I dressed and pulled on my yellow outer robe. "My stepmother intends to sacrifice my little sister at the temple dedication. I have to get her away from there." I went to the chest and took out the red wig.

The men came out from behind the loom. Yofni went to listen at the door, while Salme came to stand beside me. "Hold still," he said, and straightened the elaborate wig for me. "When will you return?"

"The moment I get her away from my stepmother." I smoothed down the sleeve my haste had wrinkled and reached for a pot of kohl. "Salme, will you take her with you tonight?"

"A child? I do not think it would be wise, Rahab."

I had no mirror, so I handed him the kohl brush. "Paint a line around my lashes." I closed my eyes. "Tezi is quick and she can be quiet. She will not slow you down very much. She is also half-Semite, like me."

The brush gently moved across my eyelid. "If we are caught, she could be killed."

"If my sister stays in Riha, my stepmother will ruin her life, out of spite against my father. My father cannot protect her. She does not know I am a harlot, and this house is no place for a child." I clenched my fists in the sides of my outer robe. "Please, Salme. Please take her. Give her a chance to live with her people. Surely someone will adopt her."

"I had thought you might wish to go with us," Salme said. "If you were to come with your sister, you could be together. No one would have to adopt her. You could be with your people, Rahab." A muscle ticked in his jaw. "You would be with me."

My mouth went dry. "I did not think captains of the army could keep harlots for themselves."

"You would not be my harlot." He looked all over my face, as if memorizing my countenance. "You would be my wife."

The room tilted for a moment as his words sank into my heart, tearing at it with their gentle claws. Jezere had told me once that she had fallen in love with my father the first time she had set eyes on him. When he had asked her to leave the house where she served to marry him, she had done so gladly. She had even denied her people and her religion to do so.

Love demands things of us, Rahab. We pay dearly for it, but if it is truly love, we do so with gladness.

I had loved my mother, and honored her by practicing an outlawed religion in secret. I loved my sister enough to keep my silence and become an outcast to protect her. To save Tezi, I would gladly send her away and never see her again. I had loved Narath, and part of me always would, for the gentleness and affection he had shown me.

I did not love Salme. I did not *know* Salme. Yet in my heart I suspected that, given the chance and more time, I would. I could easily go with him, and be with Tezi, and in time, perhaps even become his wife. I would never have to be a harlot again. I could forget that I had been. No one would stop me.

Only the promise I had made Tiamat stood in my way.

"I must stay here," I told him. "These women depend on me. I cannot abandon them."

Yofni lifted his hand, indicating we should be silent. Footsteps passed the door, and I heard Zakiti grumbling out in the hall as she trudged to the stairs.

Salme tugged me into his arms and held me against him. Against my hair, he whispered, "Have you not sacrificed enough of yourself for others? How can I leave you behind, knowing . . ."

Knowing that I might be killed in the battle to come. "Take my sister," I murmured. "She is only a little girl. She deserves a chance to live."

We all froze in place when there was a knock on the door.

"Rahab?" It was Karasbaal. "We must leave now, before the streets are impassible."

I looked up at Salme. "My sister?"

"She will go with us." Salme bent down and pressed his mouth to mine. "Be careful," he said against my lips, and then he went and hid behind the loom with Yofni.

I walked to the door and opened it. "I am ready to go."

The streets of Meshnedef were busy as merchants, citizens, and miskin came out to celebrate or take advantage of the public holiday. Because there was no red to be had, everyone wore symbols of Moloch instead. Men painted their foreheads with black horns, beat on small temple drums, or carried blazing torches. Women dressed in their finest, draping their arms and throats with clay beads and bangles painted to look like gold.

"Your kohl line is too thick," Karasbaal said, taking my arm to pull me around a pair of men arguing over possession of a frightened female slave and the jug of wine she held. "You look like Tiamat with it so dark. Did your hands shake as you applied it?"

Salme's must have, probably more from nervousness than fear. I doubted a captain of the army had much opportunity to paint a woman's eyes. "Yes."

"It does not detract, I suppose, but then, nothing does." He made a show of inspecting me. "You are a beautiful woman, Rahab. So full of emotion. I especially like how your skin glows when you are angry."

"I should light up the whole quarter, then," I said.

"I am curious to know how you will appear when you are on your knees before me. Has one of the men ever made you play bid'lem to his god?" He gazed ahead at a large, rowdy crowd forming a ring around a tavern dancer who had taken her performance into the street. "We will go through here."

He turned and went into an alley that led to the poorest section of Meshnedef. Here were the streets I had run through, trying to escape the beggars and thugs, my first day cast out from my family. How frightened I had been that day, and how little the place affected me now. Perhaps because in the months since I had learned of too many things far worse than having nothing to eat and nowhere to go.

"Your stepmother will be surprised to see you," Karasbaal said. Evidently he was determined to keep up his sarcastic form of conversation with me. "I told her that I would bring her something special. Perhaps you can persuade her to allow you to change places with Tezi."

"So you can put your hands on my sister? I think not." I pulled my arm from his grip.

"I am not so bad, you know." He chuckled at the sight of a dog chasing after a squealing, swollen-bellied child. "Your stepmother will enjoy watching us together."

"I am not making the shakab with you in front of her," I told him through clenched teeth.

"Rahab, you have not sorted it out by now? From this day forth you will do whatever I tell you. Just as Ubalnu does." He pulled me away from a drunken man vomiting in the gutter and led me through another side street away from the miskin.

"You can taunt me as much as you like later," I said. "For now I must know what to do. How do you plan to get Tezi away from my stepmother?"

"We are meeting her outside the new temple. She will have your sister with her." He gestured up toward the citadel. "I shall greet her and distract her while you take the girl. The crowd will be such that it will be easy for you two to become lost in it. You will go to the temple of Baal at the inner city gates and wait there for me."

There were so many things that could go wrong I nearly stopped in my tracks. "And this is your plan."

"It is always best to keep things simple. Do you have a better idea?" He watched me gnaw at my lip. "I thought not."

It took more precious time to make our way through the artisans' quarter and take the elevated path to the citadel. The long line of people waiting to pass through the gates did not help, either. Guards were checking each person, searching some and warning all who entered the inner city not to disrupt the solemn dedication ceremony, which would take place when the sun was directly over the temple.

"How will we know when it begins?" I heard a woman ahead of us complain to the guard.

"Listen for the drums and look for the red," the

guard told her. "There will be plenty of both when Lord Lukur brings the statue out from the inner sanctum."

Karasbaal and I passed through the gates without being stopped, and as we walked to the temple, I saw people giving me odd looks and making the sign of Moloch.

"It is your hair, dear Rahab," Karasbaal told me when he saw me frown at a matron who smiled brightly at me. "Red is a blessed color now. Anyone with hair your color is seen as an embodiment of Moloch, as well as a prospective consort for the high priest. Who knows, perhaps Lord Lukur himself will take notice of you. I wouldn't expect much profit from it. Like most rich men, he doesn't believe he has to pay for anything."

I stopped listening to Karasbaal's malicious remarks and watched the people around us, hoping to see Tezi. Many mothers were also walking to the temple. They carried swaddled infants or led small toddlers by the hand. Some looked grimly resolved, but most appeared deeply distressed. A few wept openly as they clung to their babies.

"Is he truly going to sacrifice all these children?"

"Lukur will do whatever he wishes," Karasbaal said. "Khormad has put all his faith in him. Moloch is king of Riha now."

CHAPTER
15

I had never walked through the beautiful streets of the citadel, nor viewed the grand houses of the wealthiest of Riha. It was a place I as a merchant's daughter had looked up to and had dreamed of visiting, but knew it beyond my reach.

There were no dried- or baked-brick dwellings here; the people lived in small fortresses of dressed limestone and polished cedar. Doorways were framed in rare wood inlaid with ivory and bone. Gardens and grottoes of deep cool green beckoned to the eye; there were palms everywhere.

I could not admire it too much. This was where Tiamat's mother had been cast out, and where my stepmother had insinuated herself, attending temple ceremonies so she could count herself among the best people in the city. Countless souls had been bled here, all to quench the thirst of a god who did not exist. Yet even the dubious beauty of the inner city dimmed as we arrived at the temple of Moloch.

It was not hard to miss. The entire structure had been shrouded completely in red.

I was a weaver, and I knew how much cloth it took to cover something. Here stood one of the largest buildings in the city, second in size only to the king's palace, and it had been draped from roof peak to foundation with a single layer of brilliant scarlet cloth.

For a moment I tried to imagine the scale of the loom that had been used to work such a cloth. "How did they do this?"

"If you wish to make an old whore look beautiful," Karasbaal said, "You must dress her with something that distracts the eye."

The crowd massing before the temple did not allow us to draw too close, but I spotted a seam and then another, and gradually discovered that the shroud over the temple had been stitched together of many pieces of cloth, all dyed together so that they resembled a single piece.

"So this was why he wanted all the red in the city." On closer inspection it seemed silly and wasteful to me.

"Karas!"

I heard Helsbah's voice and tore my gaze from the temple. "Where is she?" I looked around for my stepmother and my sister.

"There." He pointed to a ridiculously overdressed woman, glittering with jewels, who was leading a small girl by the hand. As they were on the other side of the crowd, he lifted his arm and waved it. At the same time, he turned me so that I could not see them. "Cover your face."

I stared at him. "I thought you wanted her to see me."

"Not this day." He pulled my veil forward until it hid me from view. "Stand away from me. She is expecting me to come alone. When her back is to you, grab the girl and leave."

A line of priests in gold and scarlet robes filed out from the sides of the temple. Each held a long white cord that led underneath the scarlet shroud. As they walked forward, the shroud began to part down the center, revealing the gilded columns at the front of the temple.

On a platform between the columns stood the high priest, Lukur, in long, trailing bloodred robes. A golden band encircled his head, a mark of the king's favor. He carried a curved golden dagger in his right hand, and a flaming torch in his left.

"Look!" someone close to us shouted, and a hand pointed up to the sky. "Moloch comes!"

A golden haze drifted across the sky from the east, moving at a leisurely pace.

That was not Moloch, I thought, studying the sky. That was a sandstorm, blowing just to the east of the city. But was it coming toward Riha, or moving to the north?

"People of Riha," Lukur shouted from the platform. "Today marks a new era in the history of the oldest and greatest city in the world. Today we become the true bid'lem of the divine god of fire, Mo-

215

loch the destroyer, and no one who threatens us will escape his inferno!"

Cheers rose from the crowd, but not as many as I expected. People were still watching the sky, some puzzled, some frightened. Everyone knew what a sandstorm looked like, but on this day many probably thought it an ill omen.

"There you are," I heard my stepmother say as she reached Karasbaal. "I thought I would never make it through this herd." She had Tezi gripped firmly by one wrist. "You must clear a path for us, Karas. I do not want to fight to be among the first to feed the god."

Tezi had been dressed in a plain white robe and wore no sandals, and her hair had been brushed out and hung over her shoulders. Her face looked pale, and there were dark circles under her dull eyes. I would have thought her drowsy, from the way she swayed slightly as she stood there, saying and doing nothing, until I realized what Helsbah had done.

Tezi had been drugged with poppy juice to keep her docile.

At that moment, I could have put my arms around my stepmother's fat neck and squeezed until her eyes popped out of her skull.

"You have not even given me a kiss hello," Karasbaal was saying to Helsbah, his voice shifting to a high, petulant tone I had never heard him use. "Come, let go of that child and embrace me. I have missed you."

"Here, in front of all these people?" My stepmother tittered. "They will think me a woman-lover."

"Well, then." He held out his hands. "Pretend I am your beloved sister."

As Karasbaal raised his arms, so did Lukur, and the rest of the temple shroud fell away. Gasps and cries rang out as the magnificent building was revealed.

It was not a new building, but an old one that had been made over to look new. I could not place it at first, and then I recalled my father pointing to its silhouette one day while complaining about the lack of tribute being paid at the temple of Baal. By taking over the temple and dedicating it to Moloch, Lukur was sending a message: the reign of Baal as godhead of the city was over.

The usual wooden asherim, used for public sacrifices, had been removed. Lukur had replaced them with gilded stone masseboth arranged in circles on either side of the platform.

I turned my attention back on Helsbah, whom Karasbaal was still charming. The moment my stepmother released Tezi and went into Karasbaal's arms, I moved forward and seized my sister from behind. To keep her from making any noise, I put a hand over her mouth and held her so as I picked her up by the waist. I huddled over and pushed through the crowd, ignoring the curious looks from people who had seen me grab my sister. There were not many, for all eyes were on the high priest and the enormous statue being rolled out of the inner sanctum.

Torches were lit and the flames danced, reflecting off the giant golden calf-headed god and leaping toward the rapidly yellowing sky.

Helsbah did not cry out until I was well away from her and Karasbaal. "Where is she? Tezi? Tezi!"

I removed my hand from my sister's mouth, turned her in my arms, and made her look at me. Her dull eyes widened as she recognized me.

"Yes, it is Rabi." I kissed her and felt her hug me with her limp arms as I draped her head with my veil. "Hold on tight, Little Sister."

If I ran from the dedication, I would be noticed, so I worked my way across the crowd instead of away from it. I glanced over at the front of the temple, where a line of people leading children had formed. The high priests took out ceremonial drums, which they began beating with the heels of their hands in loud, rapid rhythm.

To drown out the sounds of sobbing mothers, I thought, and regarded the long line of children. I was saving my sister, but who would save them? Why did their parents stand there and do nothing?

I eyed the shroud hanging from the sides of the temple, and the torches, which had oil-soaked tops that had been set aflame. I looked back to see if Helsbah was following, but saw no sign of her. Then I glanced up at the sky, which had turned a sickly yellow color—the same color it did just before a khamsin blew over the city.

"Jehovah, protect me," I muttered.

I found a stone archway leading from the temple grounds into a small row of merchant shops. All of the shops were closed in honor of the ceremony, and the street was empty. I led Tezi to a shadowed niche behind the column of the archway.

"I shall be back in a moment," I told her. "Stay here."

I did not have to get very close to the temple to do what I intended. On my way back, I took one of the torches from the wall and carried it with me. I looked no different than any of the other citizens waving them and shouting out praises for Moloch.

Lukur now stood before the statue of Moloch and was making offerings to it, calling out the name of each as he placed them in hollow spaces evidently made specially for them within the statue itself.

"Grain for the plentiful harvest," he said as he poured a sack of flour into one aperture. "Doves for the beauty of our city." He took the pair of fluttering birds from one of his priests and shoved them into a kluv before placing the small cage inside another space.

I had to push my way toward the temple, but no one objected. They were mesmerized by the offerings, which grew larger and required more effort to fit into the statue's hollow core. A ewe, a ram, and a goat were all brought forward and put inside the statue. The last, a calf, was led into the hollow base of the statue, the only space large enough to accommodate it.

The crowd and the drums fell silent when a tearful mother led a beautiful young boy, no more than four years old, up to the high priest.

"The final offering is the seed of Riha," Lukur called out as he lifted the child and placed him in a much larger kluv. Ropes strung over the statue were attached to the top of the child's cage, and the other priests began hauling it up toward the statue's outstretched arms.

Men around me looked away. Women began to weep, but the priests were too busy leading more children to the stone masseboth, where they were tied with scarlet cords.

Lukur took one of the torches and inserted it into the mouth of the statue. At once fire burst out all over the giant god, and the animals captured inside it shrieked. The child did as well, but the priests kept pulling on the ropes, drawing him closer to the flames billowing up between the statue's arms.

The boy would be burned alive.

I threw the torch then, and in the silence as it flew overhead, I shouted, "No more should die for the glory of Lukur!"

The high priest turned and looked directly at me just as my torch landed on the shroud above him, which began to burn.

People all around me gazed upon me, and I realized my veil had fallen back and my red hair was exposed. One man pointed a shaking finger at my red wig, another at my yellow outer robe.

"Baal in his outrage has cursed Moloch for stealing

his temple," a woman cried out. "He means to burn the fire god in his own flames."

Another torch was flung. More people cried out and tried to see where it landed. Suddenly the air was filled with torches as the crowd surged forward and shouted angrily. The wind picked up and fanned the flames, which spread rapidly.

"Pull it down!" Lukur shouted at his priests.

The cage and the boy dropped back down as they abandoned their ropes and went to grab at the smoldering edges of the temple shroud, which were flapping wildly as the wind rose.

The sandstorm had not turned north. We could all hear the roar as it approached the city from the east.

People snatched up their children and ran away from the temple. I did the same, heading for the place I had hidden Tezi, glancing back only once.

Lukur had the marianu, who served as the king's guards, with him now, and was shouting at them and pointing in my direction.

Karasbaal appeared beside me, and jerked me to one side, where a group of men shouting and shaking their fists at Lukur blocked us from the high priest's sight. "I said take your sister, not burn down the temple," he told me as he stripped out of his robe. "Here." He shoved the dark green robe at me. "Give me yours."

I saw Helsbah rushing up to the high priest, arms outstretched. "What are you talking about?"

He jerked the robe from my shoulders. "There is no time to talk, you stupid woman." He dressed me in his and draped his head with a length of red cloth. "Get your sister through the gates, as quickly as you can. Lukur will order them closed as soon as his wits return, and then you will be trapped here with the others and he can take his time."

"What are you doing?"

"I cannot raise your sister. The poor girl would become completely confused about men and women." He looked over his shoulder. "I would have spoiled you for all other men, Rahab. Remember that." He took off running, shouting the same words I had before. "No more should die for the glory of Lukur! No more should die!"

I started after him, intending to stop him, but he was too fast. I saw him disappear around the side of the temple, ten guards chasing him, and then turned and ran for the archway and Tezi.

Even with Karasbaal's ruse, I did not dare remain in the citadel, and we would need shelter from the storm. As soon as I retrieved Tezi from the shadows of the archway, I ran to the inner city gates. My sister was still too drugged to walk, but carrying her made me look like a hundred other mothers running from the burning temple and the khamsin.

Just after we went through, an official called out to close the gate, which created an instant riot. I heard the distant screams of women and shouts from men, but I did not stop until I reached the relative safety of the merchants' quarter.

"We will wait out the storm here," I told Tezi as I set her on her feet in front of our father's house.

"Rabi, what happened?" she asked me, sounding dazed. "Where is Little Mother?"

"I shall explain later. Come inside." I led her into the house through the kitchen. An elderly man and woman were closing the shutters to keep out the wind, and reacted with relief when they saw Tezi.

"Her stepmother said she was taking her to a neighbor's celebration," the old woman told me. "She said Master Robur would be there."

"She lied." I carried Tezi back to her room and put her to bed. "Sleep," I told my sister. "I shall wake you when the storm passes, and we will go to the house where I live."

"I can come and stay with you?" my sister murmured as her eyes closed.

I brushed the grit from her face. "For a little while."

While my sister slept, I packed what clothes Tezi would need, and took what silver I could find from my father's chest. When I came out to the kitchen, I asked the old woman to pack some food and water for a journey.

"Where are you going with the little one, mistress?" she asked, bewildered.

I told her and her husband everything: what Helsbah had planned, how she had drugged Tezi and abducted her, how I had stolen my sister back, and the fire I had set to stop Lukur's sacrifices. By the time I finished my tale, her eyes were wide and frightened.

"Tell my father exactly what I have told you," I instructed the old couple. "Say that Rahab took Tezi out of the city, to a place where she will be safe."

The khamsin lasted another two hours, but by the time the winds died down Tezi was awake and almost back to herself. All she could talk about was visiting my new home and being with me, and I let her chatter on, aware of how close I had come to losing her. I made her bathe and dress in clean robes, and went to my room to change my own. Helsbah must have taken most of my good clothing, I discovered, for all that was left in my chest were the shabbiest and oldest I had possessed.

Tezi and I left the house as soon as it the wind died down enough for us to walk outside. The storm had put an end to the citywide celebrations, and there were no patrols out yet, so we made our way to Meshnedef without difficulty.

"This is a dirty place," Tezi said, wrinkling her nose as she saw the refuse the storm had flung all over the streets. "Why do you live here?"

I was hot, tired, and almost sure that Karasbaal had sacrificed himself to save us. Setting fire to the temple shroud may have saved the children, but it would not stop Lukur. And there were Tezi, and my father, and Helsbah. "It is the only place I could live when I was cast out, Little Sister. It is not as bad as it looks."

Tezi put her arm through mine. "Nothing looks bad anymore now that we are together again, Rabi."

CHAPTER
16

I could not smuggle Tezi into the House of Palms, not in the middle of the afternoon, and there was no time to prepare the zanna for her presence. She was too young to understand what a harlot was, but her time of being a child was drawing quickly to a close.

It was time to tell her the truth.

"Tezi, when Father cast me out, I had nothing but a bald head and a servant's robe," I said as we walked through the empty market. "I did not mean to come to Meshnedef, but that was where I wandered that day. This is the part of the city where the miskin, those who have nothing, come to live."

Her eyes rounded. "You mean, beggars?"

"Beggars and thieves and harlots." I took a deep breath. "You do not know what a harlot is, but—"

"Yes, I do," Tezi said immediately. "That is what one calls a woman who sells the use of her body to men."

I stared down at her. "How did you know that?"

"Little Mother spoke of them to one of her friends, when I was listening at the door." Tezi made a face. "Her friends like to hire harlots for some of their feasts. They make them serve their husbands and the men."

"I cannot believe this." I looked up at the sky, which was turning to a more normal blue color now. "I did not know such things when I was your age."

"You did not have Little Mother around the house." She curled her fingers around mine. "If there are women like that where you live, I shall not mind it, Rabi. It is not their fault they must do such things. Little Mother said that most of them are . . ." she stopped walking.

I turned to her. "What is it?"

"You had to become a *harlot*," she whispered the word. "That is what you are trying to tell me."

I could not help smiling. "I need not tell you anything. You will work it all out on your own."

"Then it is true," she said slowly.

I nodded. "I did not wish to be a beggar, or a thief."

She gulped and looked at her sandals.

"Tezi, I am the same person I was before this happened," I lied. "It is something I do to earn my living. It is not who I am. It is not even what I wish to be."

"I know that." She peered up at me. "Is it terrible, being a harlot? Are the men kind to you? Are you paid well for it? Do they make you wear all that paint on your face?"

Of course she would have a thousand questions. In her place, I would as well. "Tezi, we will talk about it another time. For now, I must take you into the house where I live. The woman who is mistress of the house, Tiamat, took me in when I had nothing. She has been very kind to me. But she does not permit children in the house, so you cannot stay there."

"Maybe you could tell her I shall not be much trouble." She ducked her head. "I do not want to go back to Father's house. I do not like it there. I am afraid of Little Mother taking me to the temple again."

I rested my hands on her shoulders. "That is why I am sending you out of the city with two of my friends. They will take you to live with Mother's people." She began to ask more questions, but I shook my head. "It will be dark soon, and you have to leave Riha tonight. I shall come and see you when I can." *Jehovah, forgive me for all the falsehoods I am uttering.* "Come, now, we must hurry."

When we reached the House of Palms, Banune met us at the door.

"Hello," she said, smiling at Tezi before giving me a hard look. "You were not to go out today. We were worried when we found you gone and the khamsin came. Karasbaal also went out." She inspected my old robes. "Where did you get that rag?"

"The same place I found shelter from the storm.

This is my sister, Tezi," I told her. "Tezi, this is my friend Banune."

My little sister gave her a tentative smile. "Hello. Are you a harlot, too, like Rahab?"

"Yes, dear one, I am." She chuckled, surprised. "Have you come for a visit?"

"A brief one," I told her, guiding Tezi to the stairs. "After she meets Tia, she will be staying in my room. Only for the night."

Banune nodded. "I shall tell the others. Tiamat is upstairs weaving."

I remembered the flax and groaned. "I forgot, I left two bundles of flax on the roof. They must have blown all the way to Egypt."

"I took them down before the storm and put them in your room," Banune said. "Do you know where Karasbaal may have gone?"

I hoped still evading the marianu in the citadel. "I cannot say." Had Banune seen Salme and Yofni when she had gone into my room? "Did anything else happen while I was gone?"

"Ubalnu and Zakiti had a disagreement over the last of the soft cheese," Banune said wryly. "Ubalnu won."

I took my sister upstairs to meet Tiamat, who asked no questions and greeted Tezi as if expecting her. After some initial shyness my little sister began chatting to her as if she were a favorite aunt. In no time Tiamat had Tezi sitting at her vanity and playing with her wigs and cosmetics. It was then that she drew me to the side and I quietly told her everything, from Karasbaal's bargain to fleeing the inner city.

"You did a brave thing, Rahab." Tiamat glanced over at my sister. "You will have her go with them tonight?"

"Salme said they would take her." I went to the window to check the distance to the wall. "I do not think she can climb across on ropes."

"There is another way." She touched my wig. "This is full of sand. Give it to me and I shall clean it for you."

I removed the wig and handed it to her. "I meant to take better care of it." I groaned as I spotted my sister's reflection in the bronze disk and hurried over. "Tezi, what have you done?"

"I look like a harlot, too, see?" She turned and presented her comically painted face to Tiamat. "Can I stay and be with Rabi now?"

Tiamat crouched before her. "I wish you could, Little One, but this is not the place for you. Rahab tells me you are going on a journey, and you will have a whole new family waiting to meet you."

"My mother's people." She yawned. "I want Rahab to go with me."

"She is tired." I went and picked her up in my arms. "I shall take her to my room to rest. When shall we . . ." I nodded toward the window.

"As soon as the last guest leaves tonight."

I felt exhausted by the time I carried Tezi into my room and closed the door.

"It is Rahab," I said softly as I carried my dozing sister to my sleeping mat. The effects of the drug Helsbah had given her must have lingered, for she curled up and went to sleep instantly.

Salme and Yofni slipped out from behind the loom.

"You found her." Salme smiled down at Tezi. "Was she harmed?"

His smile chased all the tiredness from my limbs. "No, we reached her before she was taken to the temple." I pulled a blanket over my sister and felt the cool air from the window on my head.

"Your hair is very red." Salme's fingers teased a short piece above my ear. "It must be like fire when it grows long."

"That fire will take a few years to build." I was pleased by his compliment, though, and glad my head was no longer completely bare. "I need to prepare for our guests. When they are gone and the last patrol passes, then it will be safe for you to go over the wall."

I gave them the food I had brought from my father's house, as well as Tezi's garments, and put on my brown wig. As I prepared to change out of my shabby robes, sudden shouts and loud pounding from downstairs made me jump. The men both went to the window.

"Bring out the men," a terrible voice commanded. "We know they are here."

"City guards." Salme turned to me. "They have a priest of Moloch with them. He is dressed in golden robes."

Lukur? I went to the window to look down, but they were already moving into the house. There was no time to satisfy my curiosity, either; they would be searching the first floor even now.

I spied the damp flax Banune had left neatly piled in one corner. "Help me carry this up onto the roof."

"This is not the time to do chores," Yofni hissed.

"If you lie on the roof, I can spread it over you." I grabbed an armful of the soggy stems. "It is the only way."

The men gathered up the flax and followed me to the narrow steps leading up to the roof. I pushed the wooden cover aside and climbed out.

The roof of the house was flat, like a floor, and was usually spotted by bird droppings. Today it had been scoured clean by the khamsin. I crouched down at first, checking the top of the wall for patrols before I called softly to the men. "It is clear."

I told them to drop the flax in a pile and lie in the corner of the roof shadowed by the city wall. "This will cover you, but you cannot move," I warned Yofni as I spread the flax over him.

"What of your sister?" Salme asked before I did the same to him.

"They will have to go through me to get to her," I assured him.

He seized my wrist. "Let me go. Yofni can take what we know back to Joshua."

"If they find you, they will kill us all." I placed a swath of flax over his face. "If they take me now, do not leave Tezi behind."

I dared not linger on the roof, but climbed back down and pulled the cover back in place. The house below was very quiet, and I only heard one man's voice speaking. I looked in on Tezi, who was still asleep, and then made my way down to the first floor.

A guard stopped me at the foot of the stairs and searched me, then gave me a push in the direction of the great room. "In there."

All the other guards had crowded inside the room, and were standing around the high priest, who was helping himself to our food.

"Where are the men?" Tashish, the captain of the guard, demanded. "We know they came here."

"Some men came to see me, but I did not know they were spies," Ubalnu said, sounding bored. "They had me and left just before you came here. I saw them going toward the trader's gate. If you are quick, you may overtake them."

Several of the guards hurried out of the house, but most remained, along with the high priest.

"She may be lying," Lukur said to Tashish. "Search the house. I also want the redheaded harlot. It was she who threw the torch." He watched the rest of his men file out of the room.

"How do you know that?" Tiamat said.

"I saw you myself," I heard Lukur say as he turned his back on us and went to the wine table. "It was clever to send the eunuch in your robes to fool the guards. He was not as fast as he should have been.

His head now decorates the gate through which you escaped. Yours will join it in the morning, harlot."

Karasbaal. I closed my eyes for a moment, and then opened my mouth to answer him.

"I shall be glad to keep him company," Tiamat said, pulling off her veil. "What he did was a great hesed to me."

Tia had changed out of her elegant Egyptian garments into the simple Canaanite robes the rest of us wore. She was also wearing my red wig, and had painted her face to look more like mine. "No."

Lukur flicked a glance at me and then one of the guards, who clamped a hand on my neck and told me to be silent.

"My sisters are eager to protect me, but they knew nothing of what Karasbaal and I did." Tiamat looked over at me, and then at the other zanna, who were watching her with the same horror I felt. "They are too afraid to do anything."

"But you were not, Rahab. That is your name, is it not? Your confederate called it out before he fainted." Lukur picked up a bronze goblet. "A pity we could not revive him so that he could enjoy his execution. He slept through the entire thing."

Tiamat looked at me, and lifted her left hand to brush back a piece of red hair from her cheek. Her scarab rings glittered. "Yes. I am Rahab."

"You should not admit it so readily," Lukur said, clearly disappointed. "I might have believed you if you claimed to be another, even under torture."

"You saw me with your own eyes." Tiamat took a dagger from her robe, and drove it into her breast.

Banune shrieked and ran forward to catch her as she fell. Blood spilled down the front of her robe, and then I was beside her, holding her hand and sobbing.

"Rahab," she murmured. "I am Rahab."

"Impatient wench," Lukur said as he came to look down at her.

Tashish returned. "We found no one but a harlot asleep in a room upstairs." He sounded disgust. "She is only a child."

"A pity she has been used, or we could take her back to the temple for tomorrow's rededication ceremony." He sighed. "Take the men and search the rest of the quarter. They have to be in one of these houses." Lukur sat down and gestured to me. "You, come and pour me some wine."

I rose, Tiamat's blood on my robe, and walked over to look down at the goblets. The black scarab ring felt cold on my finger, but the stone turned easily. The powder itself dissolved as soon as I added the wine.

"Fill it to the brim," the high priest snapped. "My throat is filled with storm dust." To Banune, who was silently weeping over Tiamat's body, he said, "Drag that dead whore outside. The smell of her sickens me."

Ubalnu came and took the goblet from me. There were tears in her eyes. "I shall serve him." She brought the goblet to Lukur, who took it and sniffed the contents before taking a large swallow.

I had emptied all the powder from Tia's black ring into the cup, so it did not take long. At first Lukur paled, and then beads of sweat appeared above his upper lip.

"Where are my men?" he said, lurching to his feet. "Guards!"

Ubalnu walked over and closed the door. "They have gone to search for the spies, Priest. Do you not remember? You sent them yourself."

He clutched his stomach, and then threw the goblet of poisoned wine at her. She turned quickly and it hit the wall, splashing the last of the wine over it.

"You should have told them to stay," Ubalnu said as she began to walk toward him. "I am Rahab."

Zakiti went to Banune and touched her shoulder. She then looked at Lukur. "I, too, am Rahab."

Banune looked up, her face wet. "I . . . am Rahab." She lowered Tiamat to the floor, and stood, taking Zakiti's hand to steady herself.

Cook came in from the kitchen. She did not look old or tired now. "I am Rahab."

We formed a circle around the high priest, and moved in.

"You cannot all be Rahab," he said in a strangled whisper, turning back and forth, staggering between us. He spun around to see Arwia behind him.

"But I am Rahab," she said in her sweet voice.

Lukur faced me. "You—you make them close their mouths. Rahab is dead. She killed herself."

"No, Priest." I took off my wig. "For I am Rahab."

CHAPTER
17

"The high priest left with two marianu some time ago," Arwia told Tashish when he returned for Lukur an hour later. "They said something about spies found in the inner city. They took Rahab's body with them."

The guards searched every floor and then reported back to their captain. Lukur and the dead harlot were not in the house.

"He sends us on a fool's errand and then runs back to the king to show off a dead whore." Tashish looked disgusted. "Let him use the palace guard, then, to search for his spies." He led his men out of the house.

We took the bell in, a sign to any men who might come that the house was closed for the night. Then we stood together, six women where there had once been seven, united by something much stronger than grief.

"We will bury her beneath the palms," Banune said. "It was her wish."

Ubalnu studied her long nails, which were rimmed with blood. "What about him?"

"The enclosure will do." Arwia brushed at a small dark stain on the front of her robe. "Perhaps where the goats like to make their water."

"Yes, so they can piss on his resting place for all time," Zakiti said.

"Better to drop him down the tomb hole behind the trenchers," I said.

"I am too old for this." Cook rubbed a gnarled hand over her face and sighed. "I shall pack some food for the men." She hobbled off to the kitchen.

I scanned the faces of the other zanna, who had not been startled when I had brought down Salme and Yofni before to help us with the bodies. "You all knew about the men hiding in my room?"

"You would bring two men into this house, keep them in your room, and believe us *not* know of it?" Ubalnu asked. "I could smell them every time I passed the door."

"Go and get them out of the trees, Rahab," Banune said. "It is time they go."

I went out to the garden, and called Salme and Yofni out of the palms, where they had been hiding since taking Tiamat and Lukur up to the roof. Putting the bodies under the flax had been the only way to convince Tashish of our lie.

"It is done," I told them. "The guards have gone

back to their barracks. It is safe for you to cross now."

The two Semites insisted on carrying the bodies down from the roof, and carefully placed Tiamat outside in the garden for Banune, who wrapped her in the weaving we had taken down from her loom. Lukur's torn, battered body was dragged to the enclosure and dropped down into the old tomb shaft behind the goats' trenchers.

"Poison seems too good a death for this kelb'lim," Salme said as we shoveled dirt into the top of the tomb hole to conceal it.

"Poison did not kill him." Like Ubalnu, I, too, had blood under my nails. I looked at him. "It would have, had we given it time to."

He nodded and packed the dirt down with his sandal. For a moment, the way he stood, he looked as Narath had the last time I had seen him.

"Salme, there is something you should tell Joshua." I quickly told him everything Narath had told me about the repair of the walls and the tremor pits that had been filled in with sand. "I do not know if it can help you, but it is a weakness. Perhaps one you can make use of, if you did not already know of it."

"No, Yofni and I only saw that the walls were old and marked those which were crumbling. We could not know the nature of the repairs done to them." Salme rested a hand on my shoulder. "I thank you for telling me."

Tezi was very sleepy when I woke her, and unaware of the night's horrors. Salme carried her in his arms up to the roof and surveyed the distance from the closest edge of it to the wall.

"I could jump it, but the child cannot," he said. "We will need to string ropes and climb across. Can she hold onto my back?"

"Wait." I asked Yofni to come downstairs with me, and a short time later we returned carrying my loom between us. We lowered it to make a bridge between the house and the wall. "The weave will hold your weight, if someone steadies each side."

Salme tested it. "It will ruin your work."

"What was done here tonight is my work." I looked up at him and pushed all my feelings aside. "I am grateful to you for taking my sister out of Riha. Now I must ask one more thing of you."

"Our lives are yours," Salme told me simply.

"I know Joshua is coming to destroy Riha," I said. "Swear to me by Jehovah that when he does, you will spare this house."

Salme looked at Yofni. "Rahab, I have never said—"

"I have helped you, Salme. I have hidden you, fed you, and lied for you. I have even told you about the city's defenses. You were given sanctuary here, and that is all I ask in return. Sanctuary. When you march into Riha, spare this house and everyone in it."

"You cannot warn anyone," Yofni warned.

"She will not." Salme looked down at me. "I shall petition Joshua as soon as we return. I know he will deal kindly with you."

"The patrols might spot you from the wall, so go up to the mountains and hide there until you are sure you have not been followed," I advised. "Otherwise the king might send soldiers to attack the encampment at Gilgal."

I took Tezi into my arms to say good-bye to her. "I shall miss you, Little Sister. Stay with Salme and do as he says. He is like your uncle now."

"I shall, Rabi." She buried her face in my neck. "Come to see me soon."

I held her as long as I dared before I passed her to Yofni. Then I embraced Salme.

"I am sorry about your friend," he murmured, holding me as close as he could.

"She died to save me," I said, tears making my eyes burn. "It is a debt I can never repay."

"I know what it is like to carry that burden." He held me at arm's length. "Hang a scarlet cord from Tiamat's window, so the men know which house is yours. I shall tell Joshua how the house is marked so that no one attacks it."

I held Tezi one more time as Salme jumped over to the wall, and then handed her to Yofni and steadied my side of the loom as he carefully walked across the weave to the wall. Only when they disappeared over the side did I release the breath I had been holding.

I stood up and looked at my loom. The weave

was still strong, and so was I. Salme would keep his promise.

The disappearance of High Priest Lukur, it was said, created more panic in the citadel. A punishment sent as the din of Dagon, the Canaanite king of the gods, for Lukur's blasphemy in attempting to set Moloch above Baal. The temple Lukur had remade was still smoldering, for the interior was largely wood and the stone walls acted like a kiln.

On the day after the khamsin, the statues inside the temple must have melted, for molten gold poured out of the inner sanctum. The gold ran into the streets, badly burning anyone foolish enough to try to touch it, and people began calling it Dagon's tears. When something caused the gold to turn red as blood—stores of dye hoarded in the temple, no doubt—the citizens panicked. The king tried to maintain order by keeping the inner city gates closed, but even the fierce marianu were overpowered by the sheer numbers of people frantic to get away from the burning, bleeding temple of Moloch.

The tremor that came that afternoon turned panic into terror. Hundreds fled the city, most on foot, taking only what they could carry. At last Khormad sent down an order to barricade the outer city gates, and Riha became its own kele.

Whispers of the Semite army spread as much as Dagon's tears. Men came to the House of Palms, not for women but to talk where they could not be overheard by the city guards. Akhete brought the news that the Semites had somehow convinced their god to completely block the flow of the Jordan for an entire day, so their army was able to cross simply by walking across the dry riverbed.

"That is ridiculous," Darbas sputtered. "A god cannot divert a river."

Akhete glanced in the direction of the citadel. "They say the temple that burns is not cursed by Dagon, but the One God of the Semites. That He snatched up the high priest from the streets of Riha, and will do the same to all of us."

Banune's grief over Tiamat did not abate, and she spent many hours sitting in the garden next to the place where we had buried our friend. We could not mark the grave with any stone or memorial, but she planted some flowers and herb plants there.

I went to her the second day after the Semites left and sat with her. "It is beautiful out here today."

"It is hot, and the flies are everywhere." She glanced sideways at me. "I am well, Rahab. You need not watch over me."

"You are pale, you do not eat or sleep, and you forgot to bake the lehem this morning." I studied the hem of my sleeve. "You do nothing, in fact, but complain."

"I have not said a word," she flared. "Not a single word."

"Someone very wise once told me that one does not have to speak to complain." I regarded her. "Now, must I go through making you slop the goats

242

and say all those other things, or will you come into the house and bake lehem with me?"

Her pretty amber eyes filled with tears. "It is just that . . . I cannot believe she is gone. She is the only person I have ever loved who loved me in return."

Banune, who never leaned on anyone, rested her head against my shoulder. I slipped my arm around her, offering wordless comfort, for there were no words that could heal her wounded heart.

"Rahab."

I looked up to see Robur standing just beyond the garden. His robes were torn and he looked dreadful.

Banune eyed him. "A patron, this early?"

"No." I patted her shoulder and rose to my feet. "My father." I gestured for him to come into the garden, which he did with reluctance. "Did the old couple give you my message about Tezi?"

Banune gave my father a polite smile and slipped back into the house.

He nodded. "They also told me what Helsbah did. I owe you a large debt, Daughter." He hesitated, and then asked, "Where did you send Tezi? I would go and be with her as soon as they permit people to leave the city again."

"You would not be welcome where she is," I told him flatly. "She is with Mother's people."

"Your mother was a Maon," Robur said, frowning. "I know many people there. Why would I not be welcome?"

"Mother was not Maon. She only told you that to placate you, and to hide the truth. She was Semite."

My father's shock was visible. "What nonsense do you speak? Jezere was not a Semite."

"Mother was the daughter of a Semite shepherd, Ahabel, and his first wife, Tezina. Her parents died in a plague, and she had no kin to support her, so she became a servant in the house of Ahabel's master."

"I do not believe you."

"You should," I told him in flawless Semite. "She taught Tezi and me how to speak her language, how to worship her god, and how to carry on the traditions that were precious to her." I smiled and repeated myself, this time in Canaanite.

As I suspected, hearing me speak in the Semite tongue convinced him as nothing else would. "Why did she not tell me?" he demanded. "It would have made no difference to me. I loved her."

"She did not tell you because she loved you." I sighed. "She would be glad that you know now. I think she never liked lying to you."

"You sent your sister to the Semites." He paled. "What will they do to her if she tells them I am a Canaanite?"

I had expected him to shout at me for taking her, not to worry over her safety. But my father had never hated the Semites as other Rihans did, and perhaps it truly did not matter to him that Jezere had been one of a much-hated race.

"They know. It does not matter to them. They will care for her and protect her." I thought of Helsbah, and my heart hardened again. "Have you heard from your wife? Perhaps now that Tezi and I are gone, she will be happy in your home."

"That cannot be." His shoulders slumped. "Khormad had Helsbah and her brother arrested, along with the other followers of Moloch, and thrown in the kele. It is said that they will soon be put to death in an offering to Dagon."

So they would, but not by the king of Riha. "I am sorry." For him, I was. Helsbah I yet wished a slow and painful death.

My father gave me a strange look. "Why did you not go with Tezi?"

"I made a promise to stay here and protect this house." I glanced up at Tiamat's window. I would have to hang the cord soon, for the Semites would surely be marching on Riha any day now. I faced my father. "She will be well, and so will I. You should leave the city if you can." I could not tell him more than that and keep my word to Yofni and Salme.

"This is my home, and these my people." Robur fumbled for a moment and produced a small purse. "I have sold the shop. This is your share of what it brought." Before I could speak, he added, "Do not tell me you have not earned it. Your weaving—yours and your mother's—made me a wealthy man."

I accepted the silver. "I thank you."

He eyed the house. "If you ever wish to leave—if you would care to visit an old man now and again, I would be glad to welcome you into my home." He turned to go.

"Father." I wished I could trust him enough to tell him about the coming attack. But my promise to Salme and Yofni had to be kept. "If anything bad happens—if there is a threat against the city—will you come here, to my house? I shall need you." It was all I dared say.

"If I can, I shall come." He gave me a miserable smile. "Farewell, Daughter."

Another tremor struck late that night, and I woke in the darkness to find my face covered with dust from the ceiling.

"Rahab." Banune came in carrying an oil lamp. "Are you hurt? No, I can see that you are not. That was a bad one."

The two of us checked on the other zanna, who were only frightened by the violent shaking, and then we inspected the house. Tremors often caused walls to crack and ceilings to fall, but the House of Palms was sturdy, and we found no significant damage.

It was when we went upstairs to the roof to see if any fires had started in the rest of the quarter did we see the hundreds of flames moving toward Riha.

"Demons," Banune gasped, clutching my arm.

"Torches," I told her, looking out at the moving, shadowy mass that surrounded the flames. "The Semites have come."

We stood on the roof for an hour, watching the army as it split in two and surrounded the outer city walls. They moved in an eerie silence, taking up positions well away from the battlements. One tight group brought forward a strange glowing box supported by two poles and carried by four men. A man walked behind it, and the wind carried the soft sound of his chanting to us.

"Is that a bone box?" Banune whispered.

"I think it is the Ark." Dread squeezed my heart into a small knot. "The laws handed down by Jehovah to my people are kept in it."

"They could not write them on a scroll?" she asked. When I looked at her, she said, "It would be easier to carry."

"It is a long story, and the patrols will be alerted soon. We should go back inside." I remembered the sign Salme had told me to display. "I need some scarlet cord to hang from Tiamat's window. Salme said they would not attack our house if I marked it so."

"They will never get past the first of the outer walls." Banune did not sound convinced. "Besides, you cannot."

"Tiamat would not object," I assured her. "In fact, she saw this coming, and made me promise to save the zanna and the house."

Banune's expression softened. "So that is why you would not go with your sister and the men. But that is not what I meant. You cannot hang a scarlet cord from Tiamat's window because there is no scarlet in the house."

"Of course there is. I have a belt that will . . ." I abruptly recalled that the guards had confiscated my red robes. "There has to be something scarlet in the house."

We searched, first through our belongings, then through the skeins of wool and flax Tiamat and I had, but the guards had done their work well.

"I have robes in every color you could wish," Arwia said as she opened her chest to search it. "But none red, and no red dye."

"Pomegranates," I said after we had checked with the other zanna, who like Arwia had every garment in all colors except red. "I can stain some light wool with the juice."

"Zakiti ate the last of them a few days ago." Banune went into the pantry. "Cook has no madder root."

"This is ridiculous." I went out into the garden, but the only flowers that had not yet withered had small, dark blue blooms. None of the herbs we grew would produce a red color. I stood with my hands in fists, staring at the wall that was the only thing between us and the Semite army.

Banune came and touched my arm. "We can do no more tonight. Let us go back to sleep, Rahab. To-morrow we will go to market; they will surely have something there we can use."

"The markets are closed, by order of the king." We could go from house to house and beg, but given the new hatred against Moloch, I suspected such a request might make the frightened people of Riha summon the city guard, who would then arrest us as worshippers of the fire god.

"We only need a little," Banune said, her voice frustrated. "Enough to make a cord."

Before Lukur had perverted it, red had been my favorite color. I still regretted the loss of the lovely red robes that Tiamat had given me. I stared at the place where we had buried her.

Tia, who had worn a red wig to save my life.

"We could open Tia's grave," Banune said slowly, guessing my thoughts. "She is still wearing it."

"No, we will not disturb her." I knew what I had to do, and I turned to her. "Come inside."

Banune and I did not sleep that night. In the morning, I went up to Tiamat's room, and pulled up the shade covering the window.

City guards and marianu from the citadel lined the battlements of the wall behind the House of Palms. Each carried a javelin and khopesh; many also had clubs and bows. Patrols in chariots raced through the streets, warning the citizens of Meshnedef that the city was under siege and to stay indoors.

I tied the ends of the long scarlet cord Banune and I had made to the shade, and lowered it so that the loop hung on the outside of the house. I then walked out to the garden and looked up. The cord appeared to be a part of the shade hanging out of the window. The bright red color of it made it easy to see.

It was all I had to protect us—that thin red cord— and for a moment I wanted to weep. *Keep your promise to me, Salme.*

While the other zanna slept, Cook and I went through the stores.

"Enough to feed us for another moon, a little longer if we are careful," Cook said after we had surveyed our supplies. "Then we will have to start butchering the animals."

"I shall bring them inside. They will be safer if we keep them in the great room." I saw the fear in her eyes. "Be calm, Cook. I am a Semite, and I have faith Jehovah will protect us."

"Your god will not feed us." She trudged back to the cooking pit.

I cleared the furniture out of the great room, and carried in hay to cover the floor. Leading the goats and sheep inside was a tedious process, as I could only manage one at a time.

As we passed through the side door, the old billy goat tried to kick me, and I was tempted to swat his flank. I came to face him. "Semites like goat meat in their stew as much as I do."

He chuffed out some air but followed me docilely into the great room.

The sounds of the animals in the house woke everyone but Banune, who was sleeping off her labors from the night. Ubalnu laughed when she saw what I had done.

"Not much difference between them and the usual lot, is there?" She clapped me on the shoulder. "We should become shepherds."

Arwia looked scandalized. "To chase after them through the grass and the dirt? I thank you, no."

Zakiti tugged me aside. "Why did you bring the goats and sheep inside?"

"The Semites have surrounded Riha," I told her. "If it is a long siege, the guards or other people may try to steal them for food."

"As you say." She regarded the two little kids and their pregnant mother with a sober look. "If this goes on for a long time, we may have to eat them, will we not?"

"It may only be a matter of days before it is decided." I looked at my ring. While searching for something to use to make the cord, I had found some packets of powder in Tiamat's chest. One had been marked with the drawing of a black scarab. I had been tempted to give the other zanna some of the poison, just in case. "We will be well," I said, more to convince myself than Zakiti.

CHAPTER

18

Once the animals were fed and settled, I went up to the roof to keep my own watch; yet as the day wore on, the Semites did nothing. Only when the sun was overhead did a group come out of the encampment and approach the city's first outer wall.

Two lines of heavily armed soldiers came first, followed by seven men, dressed in the fine linen robes of priests. The holy men each carried a large trumpet made from a ram's horn. Behind the priests, four other men in different ceremonial robes carried the golden-lidded ark hanging from two poles.

The priests lifted their trumpets and blew them as if making a signal. The group then began to walk parallel to the outer wall, moving as if they meant to walk around the entire city.

The sound of the trumpets carried long and loud through the stillness of the city, and the guards on the wall tensed. Some lifted their weapons as if prepared to strike back. But the Semites were too far away, and they did nothing to attack the city.

What are they doing? It seemed almost more like a religious ritual than an act of war.

People climbed out onto the roofs of houses around ours to see what was happening. Some laughed at the sight of the Semites marching around the city, but others hurried back into their houses. I heard some of the marianu on the wall shout out taunts to the Semites, telling them to take their stolen gold back to Pharaoh and beg to be his slaves again.

Ubalnu, bearing a skin of wine and a basket of food, came out onto the roof. "If you stay up here all day your skin will turn as red as your hair."

My lips twitched. "True." I looked at the basket she handed me. "I am not hungry."

"Neither am I, but I have already puked this morning, so it is safe to try." She selected a wedge of cheese and bit into it. "I am pregnant."

"What?" I thought immediately of Karasbaal. "Not by—"

"No. Akhete." She made a face and put the cheese back in the basket. "I have not used any linens with him."

I was still trying to absorb the shock of learning that Ubalnu of all people would be a mother. "You *wished* to have his child?"

"He is the best looking and least stupid of the men who come here. Well, perhaps old Hlavat has far more wits, but he will not make the shakab with me.

I am beautiful and clever, and with Akhete as sire, our child is likely to be the same." She gave me a bland look. "Stop staring at me like that."

I smiled. "Karasbaal would have loved this. He would have never stopped tormenting you about it, anyway."

"You know something amusing? Akhete may have given me this child, but I think of this more as Karasbaal's. As if it were to replace the one we might have had, had he not been cut." She took a drink from the water jug and looked out at the guards leaning over to hurl insults at the Semites. "I want this child to live, Rahab. *I* want to live, and be a mother, and have a house, and a garden, and all the things a harlot can never have."

"So do I." I wanted my father and my sister. I wanted Salme. Would I ever see any of them again?

"I shall start with the child." She handed me the jug. "There is a man downstairs. He says he is your father. Should I send him away?"

"No." Relief flooded through me. "I asked him to come here if there was trouble." I gathered up the food and went back inside the house with her.

My father was in the kitchen, sitting at the table and listening to Cook grumble as she cleaned out the cooking pit. He stood and smiled when he saw me.

"Father, I am glad to see you. I was worried." I came and took his hands. "The Semites are just outside the city now."

"That is why I came. I had hoped you and I could leave together, but the barricades are being enforced,

and there is no one who will even discuss a bribe."
His smile wavered. "Helsbah and her brother were
executed this morning. The last of my servants have
abandoned me. But for you, I am all alone now.
Come home, Rahab."

"I cannot leave my friends," I said carefully, "but
you might stay here with me, Father."

"Stay here?" He looked around the kitchen. "In a
house of harlots."

"In my home," I corrected. "Please, I know it is
much to ask of you, but I would like you to be here
until this siege ends."

"We could use a man's strong back around this
place," Cook put in for good measure. "Especially if
we have to butcher our animals. Not one of these
women has the stomach for it."

Neither did my father, from the look on his face.
"I have never, that is, I do not know . . ." Robur
made an exasperated sound. "What do I care if this
is a house of harlots? It is not as if you are murderers,
or traitors."

I caught Cook's eye. "No, it is not as if we are.
Come, Father, I shall show you to your room."

Joshua's strange siege of Riha continued, and on
the next day the same group of soldiers and priests
carried out the ritual of blowing their horns and
walking around the city with the ark. They did nothing more, and nothing less. They only did it once, at
midday, exactly as they had before, and then on the
third day they did it again.

I went up each day to bear witness to the Semite midday procession. Sometimes one or two of the other zanna went with me; once my father came, and held my hand as we watched the Semites carry the ark around Riha.

People, disturbed by the strange tactic, stayed locked in their homes. The few who dared venture out were quickly chased back indoors by the city guard, who were now patrolling the streets and walls without rest.

The silence of the city became as oppressive as the growing sense of doom.

I and the other zanna kept busy at the House of Palms. Since we had no men coming to the door at night, we began to linger over our evening meal and work together doing tasks that we had once performed alone.

Robur took over caring for the animals, at first to keep his distance from the other zanna, but gradually he became accustomed to their personalities and even began to talk more openly at meals. Although he was a man, the other women treated him with a combination of warmth and respect that they might have shown their own fathers.

On the sixth day of the siege, just after the Semites performed their daily march, a small tremor struck the city. It was only strong enough to rattle a few doors, but it seemed to seize the city in a grip of terror. A cold wind rose, wailing through the empty streets, and died away just after sunset.

"It is unnerving, what they do," my father said

over the evening meal that night. "Each time I know it is time for the trumpets, I go still, and yet each time I hear them, I am startled and afraid."

I checked the cord in the window every day, for it had become my only talisman against what was to come. That night, as I stood at Tiamat's window, I knew the time was upon us. How I knew, I could not say, but I stood and prayed that Jehovah would watch over Salme. As a captain, he would be among the first to attack the city. Then I asked Him to spare my father and the other zanna, and went to bed. I did not sleep, but I felt comforted, as if Salme were there with me, holding me in his arms.

On the seventh day of the siege, I alone went up to the roof to witness the blowing of the trumpets. Robur had offered to come with me, but I asked him to stay downstairs with the women.

"This is the day, Father," I said to him. "We must be ready." When he asked me how I knew, I only kissed his cheek and went upstairs.

The armed soldiers came out of the Semite encampment, and the seven priests, and the four bearing the ark. The trumpets sounded louder and longer than I had ever heard them before, and they began their march around the city. They did not stop this time after making one trip around the walls. They kept marching, and the priests blew the trumpets again.

Seven times they made the trip around Riha.

After the seventh procession, the priests turned to face the city and blew their horns one final time. The sound of the horns was like the scream of a giant, and then something followed it, a sound I had never heard, a thousand shouts from the Semite encampment, shouts from the men who were walking toward the walls, their swords and clubs ready, the very ground rolling beneath their feet as a terrible tremor went before them, gripping the city in a fist of earth and shaking it with ceaseless fury.

Huge balls of fire appeared in the air, seemingly out of nowhere. They struck the guards patrolling the walls and sent their flaming bodies tumbling backward. They flew over the guards' heads to land on the roofs of houses and in the streets.

The earth around the city began to disappear into deep, dark holes. Then, before my unblinking eyes, the walls all around the city—every wall in Riha— began to fall. Walls that were ten and twenty and thirty feet high collapsed, not crumbling but tumbling over, as if pushed by some mighty unseen hand. As they landed, they made the most horrendous sound, deep and bone-shaking, as a giant stomping across the land would make with his footsteps.

"Rahab." Banune helped me to my feet, and held onto me as the air filled with shattering stones and screaming men. She had to shout for me to hear her. "It is a tremor. Come inside."

"It is not a tremor." I looked back to see thousands of Semites moving into the city, and the clash of swords as the city guard that had not been crushed in the fall of the walls stumbled through the rubble toward them. "Jehovah has come into Riha."

The screams began shortly after the walls fell.

My father barred the doors, and sent the zanna upstairs to wait in Tiamat's room. I went to the kitchen to get food and water, and Cook flatly refused to leave her cooking pit.

"Let them come in." She brandished a blade. "I shall make Semite soup for the evening meal."

My father, who came into the kitchen and heard this, made an exasperated sound and plucked the blade from her hand. Ignoring her complaints, he picked her up in his arms and carried her upstairs.

I followed, trying to block out the sound of stone falling and men fighting.

The zanna were like spirits, wandering about Tiamat's room without a sound. I knew of no words to comfort them, not when we could clearly hear people dying all around us. When my father went to pull aside the shade to see what was happening outside, I stopped him.

"No, Father." I drew him away. "Do not look."

We remained inside Tiamat's room all that long, terrible day. Gradually the sounds of voices disappeared, and then all we heard was the crackle of fires and the rumble of the smaller tremors, which never seemed to cease.

It was sunset when they came for us.

Most of the zanna were dozing, so only my father

and I heard the sound of someone moving down-stairs; then one of them called out to me.

"Rahab."

It was Salme's voice.

For a moment I could not move, so vast was my relief; then I went to my father, who was standing by the door, his dagger ready to strike anyone who tried to enter.

"It is one of the men who took Tezi out of the city," I told him. "Stay here. I shall go to speak to him."

Salme and Yofni were waiting for me at the bottom of the stairs. Both of them were covered with soot and blood, and Yofni had a deep gash across his brow that was still bleeding.

"We are burning the city and everything in it," Salme said. "You must come with us now. You will not be harmed. Joshua has given me his word that you will be given safe passage. Bring only what you need."

"My friends and my father come with me." He nodded. "I shall bring them down. Tezi?"

"She is at Gilgal with my family." He tried to smile. "She has been a joy to my mother, and works as hard as any grown woman in the camp. She misses you."

Salme and Yofni stayed with us as we left the house. The darkness hid some of the destruction, but fires still burned, and more were being lit. We could not walk more than a few steps without seeing the body of a guard or a Rihan. Blood painted everything; so much of it that it might have been a ghastly red shroud fashioned by Jehovah and thrown over the city.

I looked up and saw the citadel ablaze, fires burning in every dwelling, every business, and every temple. The king's palace burned more brightly than any of them.

My father walked between Arwia and Cook, his arms around each of them, guiding them through the nightmare labyrinth that had once been the streets of Meshnedef. When we finally approached the twin piles of broken stone that had once been the city gate, I glanced back but could see only one wall—or a portion of one—that had not fallen.

The one wall that still stood in Riha was the wall that Salme and Yofni had crossed, the wall that stood behind the House of Palms.

We were permitted to camp in the hills just outside the city and were given all we needed to make us comfortable. Salme and Yofni posted three men to guard our small camp before they returned to their work.

"Why do they not take anything?" Ubalnu asked me as we built a fire and prepared a meal. "They took the city; they have the right to everything in it."

"Only the silver and gold, and the vessels of bronze and iron will be taken," one of the men guarding us said. "They will be put into the treasury of the house of Jehovah. Everything else is to be burned." He looked at the fires burning in the distance.

"But that is foolish," Ubalnu argued. "You could settle here. Many people have, for thousands of years. This could one of your first cities."

"Joshua has cursed Jericho," the guard told her. "Any man who rebuilds it shall lay its foundation with his firstborn, and shall set up its gates with his youngest."

Ubalnu spread a hand over her belly. "That is a vicious curse."

"The will of Jehovah is not gentle thing," I said, earning a look of respect from the guard.

When our meal was finished, I felt a need to separate myself from the others, and walked a short distance from the camp. It was impossible to avoid looking upon the ruins of Riha. I could smell the smoke from the fires that were still raging through it.

As my sins might have devoured my soul.

I looked up and saw a few stars shining through the haze of destruction. Hope overcame the crushing guilt. My mother had taught me that all I need do for forgiveness from the One and True God was to ask for it, and so I did.

"Jehovah, I should never have become a harlot. I can see that now. No matter how necessary it seemed, it was a grievous sin against You, and everything my mother taught me. I should have found another way." I closed my eyes tightly. "I promise You, Great Redeemer, that I will live life very differently now. You will never have to do to me what you have done to Riha. Only forgive me for taking so long to see the truth of it."

I walked back to camp and joined the others by the fire. They were talking of where we would go, and what we would do. My father suggested that it would be better not to petition to join the Semites, but to obtain their permission to live on one of the abandoned farms in the hills, where we would have adequate shelter and could care for ourselves.

"It will be difficult at first," Robur warned, "but we can grow what we need and stay out of their way."

"We will need goats and sheep," Cook said. "You cannot grow them."

In the morning I woke at dawn and asked one of the guards if I could be taken to see Salme. He escorted me to the encampment, which was busy with soldiers packing up and preparing to move on to the next objective.

Salme met me outside the commander's tent. He had not bathed or changed out of his leather battle armor, and his shoulders sagged with exhaustion. "Rahab, I meant to come up and see you."

I stared for a long moment at the smoldering blackened ruin that had been the city of my birth.

"It would have happened no matter what you or I did," he said quietly.

"I want my sister back," I told him. "My father came out of the city with us, and while he is not a Semite, he is a decent man. He and I shall raise her to be a good woman. We would also like to take one of the farms in the hills for ourselves. We will live in peace and cause no trouble."

An old man came out of the tent as I said this. He wore no special robes, and was a foot shorter than Salme. He had a head of silver-black hair, a weathered, grim face, and the eyes of a hungry hawk.

"Salme." His voice snapped rather than beckoned. "Who is this woman?"

"My lord Joshua." Salme turned and bowed with his hand over his heart. "This is Rahab, the woman who sheltered us in Jericho."

I did not want to look into those dark, merciless eyes, but I did so. "Lord Joshua." I bowed my head for a moment.

"You are the harlot." He inspected me as if I were one of his troops.

"I *was* a harlot," I corrected him. "With your permission, my family and I would like to try farming instead. If you have not burned all of the farms yet."

Salme cleared his throat rather desperately.

"Not all." Joshua did not smile—he was not a man, I guessed, who smiled at all—but some of the fierceness left his gaze. "I think farming an ambition more worthy of a daughter of Jehovah." He glanced at Salme. "See to it that she is given whatever she and her family need."

"I shall, my lord." Salme bowed again. When Joshua strode off, he let out a deep breath. "You are braver than I am."

"I doubt that." I felt drained of all emotion. "I had better go. I thank you for saving us, Salme."

"This farm, you will stay there?" he asked as he walked out of the camp with me.

"I think traveling through Canaan will be difficult for some time." I tugged at my wig. "I have nowhere else to go."

"You do not have to wear this anymore." Before I could stop him, Salme pulled the brown wig from my head. "Rahab—what—"

I touched my head, which was completely bald. "You said to hang a scarlet cord out of the window. My hair was the only red thing left in the house. I shaved it off and Banune spun it with a little flax to make the cord."

"I did not know." He helped me put the wig back in place. "I am sorry."

"Hair is like hope; it always comes back." I looked up at him. "You do not want to be a soldier forever, do you?"

"When the land is ours, and Joshua has no more need of me, I think I shall put away my sword," he told me, taking my hand in his. "Farming is a worthy ambition, I am told."

I smiled down at our joined hands. "So it is."

Glossary of Terms

[*Author's note: the terms used in this novel were derived from several different languages, including Canaanite, Hebrew, Aramaic, and Urgartic. I have removed certain punctuation and spelled them in such a way to make them reader-friendly.*]

Ayin-yada: to watch intimacy
Asherim: wooden posts in Canaanite temples, used
        for sacrificial rituals
Astarte: Canaanite goddess; Queen of Heaven
Baal: Canaanite fertility god
Beqa: unit of monetary weight, equal to one-half sheqel
Bet: house
Bet ab: the house of one's father
Bid'lem: servant of the gods (sacred term)
Boset: shame
Dagon: Canaanite godhead; "father" of all Canaanite gods
Din: judgment

Hapiru: nomadic raiders

Hazrat: courtesan; plural: hazrata

Hesed: kindness

Hokhmah: wisdom

Hokhmah nisteret: hidden wisdom

Jehovah: the god of the Semites

Khamsin: sandstorm

Kelb'lim: dog of the gods (profane term)

Kele: jail

Khopesh: a sickle-shaped sword

Kiatta immadi: literally, "for you are with me"

Kluv: cage

Lehem: bread

Marianu: elite Canaanite warrior caste; king's guard

Masseboth: stone pillars in Canaanite temples, used for sacrificial rituals

Meloyikah: an edible Egyptian vegetable that is also a source of jute fiber

Mina: monetary weight, equal to sixty sheqels

Mirii: Canaanite underworld

Miskin: poor, miserable

Moloch: Canaanite god of fire

Mut'a: euphemism for a specific type of prostitution; a temporary marriage in which time with a "wife" is purchased with money

Qedesh: holy prostitutes who serve in the temples of Baal, Astarte, and Moloch

Riha: native name for the city of Jericho

Shakab: the sexual act

Taliya: garlic fried with salt and coriander

Tiph'eret: splendor, pleasure

Usfur: safflower

Zanna: caregiver; a Canaanite euphemism for prostitute

Zonah: the Semite word meaning prostitute; plural: zonot

Discussion Guide

1. In *Rahab's Story*, Rahab was falsely accused of witchcraft and violence, which resulted in her being made an outcast. She accepted this decision in order to protect her sister. What would you have done in her place? How might Rahab have better protected herself against the consequences of her stepmother's animosity toward her?

2. Prostitution has existed in some form or another among all civilizations at least since recorded history began. Presently some societies have legalized prostitution and regulate it, but most simply turn a blind eye to it. Do you agree with the legalization of prostitution? What measures can be taken to improve the lives of prostitutes? Should prostitutes have the same rights under the law as other women?

3. Among Canaanites, harlotry during Rahab's time was considered a respectable profession for

women who had no other means of support. In most cases, it was all that kept outcast women from starvation. Despite this, after becoming a harlot, Rahab suffers from guilt and self-condemnation. If you were faced with her circumstances, how would you feel? Is it better to starve with honor than live with shame?

4. There is evidence that some Canaanite tribes, like those depicted in this novel, actively practiced child sacrifice. In the Bible, God asks Abraham to sacrifice Isaac, his only son, as a demonstration of his faith. What is the difference between the two types of sacrifice? Could the story of Abraham and Isaac also be considered a condemnation or warning against pagan child-sacrifice rituals?

5. Community security has always been a concern to every society, and ancient Canaanite cities like Jericho were often fortified by walls to keep out invaders and to protect their citizens. These fortifications, however, were often made vulnerable by earthquakes, flooding, and other forces of nature. What is the modern equivalent of the walls of Jericho in your community, if any? How can you personally better protect your family and home?

6. Joshua sent spies into Jericho to scout the city's defenses; yet when God promised Joshua that He would bring down the walls of Jericho, Joshua

believed Him and followed His instructions to the letter. What other leaders have relied on their faith as well as their military expertise to make strategic decisions? Do you consider faith an effective weapon? An effective defense? Discuss the benefits and drawbacks of faith in the military.

7. Many biblical scholars compare the immoral civilization that existed in Rahab's Jericho to many of our modern society. Does widespread immorality condemn an entire society? What happens to a society after it loses all moral restraint? Does the majority have the right to determine the moral standard for everyone in society?

8. After wandering in the wilderness for forty years, Joshua led the Israelites into Canaan, the land God promised them. The settlement of Canaan by the Jews, however, required the use of force against Canaanite cities like Jericho. How does this period parallel the creation of the State of Israel in 1948? Are the ancient Canaanites comparable to modern-day Palestinians?

9. Canaan was under Egyptian rule during the Israelite conquest and settlement. Egyptian Pharaohs demanded so much tribute from Canaan that they nearly beggared the territory; yet when Canaanite kings petitioned for Egyptian help against the Israelites, Egypt gave them only empty promises. Had Egypt joined in the fight

against the Israelites, would it have made a difference at Jericho? How would history have changed if the Egyptians had driven the Israelites out of Canaan? Compare this alternative scenario to Israel's Six-Day War of 1967.

10. Rahab, a direct ancestor of King David and Jesus Christ, acted on her faith to protect the Hebrew spies and help Joshua during his conquest of Jericho. How does Rahab illustrate the concept of active faith? Does risking everything to remain true to faith redeem someone who has a sinful past?

Recommended Reading

Kenyon, Kathleen M. *Digging Up Jericho: The Results of the Jericho Excavations 1952–1956*. New York: Frederick A. Praeger, Inc., 1957. ISBN Number: 51-12697

Ruby, Robert. *Jericho*. New York: Henry Holt and Company, Inc., 1995. ISBN Number: 0-8050-2799-8

Shanks, Hershel and Benjamin Mazar, eds. *Recent Archaeology in the Land of Israel*. Washington, D.C.: Biblical Archaeology Society, 1984. ISBN Number: 0-9613089-2-3

Romer, John. *Testament: The Bible and History*. William S. Konecky & Associates, Inc., 2004. ISBN Number: 1-56852-489-7

Keller, Werner. *The Bible as History*. Translated from the German by William Neil. Barnes & Noble Books, 1990. ISBN Number: 1-56619-801-1

Read on for a preview of
Ann Burton's next Women of the Bible novel

Jael's Story

A month I had lived in my husband's tent, in which most nights he took me to his bed, and I kept myself from crying by forcing myself to remember what would happen if I did. But my silence pleased him no more than my tears, and still he shouted at me, or slapped me, and always told me I was worthless.

Days were better, for by day I had the companionship and friendship of my new sisters, and they had known my hurt and knew as well the easing of it. We shared work: preparing food, weaving and sewing and mending, tending the two boys, carrying water, and dyeing and spinning. In work I found great comfort, for nothing more fully frees the mind from worry and pain than doing something necessary. And we shared the songs we sang in the tent as we worked, and the tales we told to each other, and our laughter.

Early one morning I rose and gathered our water jars to take to the well, for I was youngest and strongest, and without a child who needed my attention. The four pretty clay *kaddim*, decorated with graceful birds in red and black, I set in a neat row. I liked them; we had the same sort of jars in my parents' home, painted with similar birds in red and black. I would need to make four trips to the well, for I could only carry one of the jugs at a time. Empty, they are quite light. Full, they are such a burden I feel like an ill-used ox, and sometimes, balancing one on my head, I think I might be crushed beneath the weight of it. But I did yearn to leave early for my own reasons, too. Several other young wives would be at the well at daybreak drawing their water for the day, and if I got there while they were there, they told stories about their lives as new wives that made me laugh. I talked sometimes about Talliya and Pigat to them, but never spoke of my husband.

My mother always said, "Kind words spread outward like ripples on water, but ill words follow you home." I had no wish to be followed home by any ill words I might say about my husband.

But as I was lifting the tent flap, I heard Heber outside, arguing with a man whose voice I had never heard before. It was a rich, deep voice, and managed to be both calm and angry.

I did not step out, but stood there, a water jug in my arms, and listened.

"I have already paid you, and you promised me that you would have my sword ready for me this day!"

I peeked out the flap to see my husband standing

next to his forge facing a stranger, his face dark with anger. "I am pressed to the working of iron for a king. Who are you that you would demand of me that I set aside the king's iron sword, that I could make your bronze one?"

The young man flushed. He was, I thought, quite handsome. His black hair hung long and thick and curling, pulled back to the nape of his neck; his flashing eyes were black as anthracite, his nose strong, his mouth firm and well shaped. He had a young man's leanness, too, with broad shoulders and a tapering waist and sturdy, finely-muscled legs. His was a young man's beard, not yet the long, thick beard of an elder, and his robes were white, and fringed in blue in the Israelite fashion.

"I am Levi of Kadesh and know only that I am not a king, but I paid you long months ago for a new sword. And that the last time I came to take ownership of it, you told me it was not yet ready, but that it would be ready today. I know, too, that a man's word is his word, whether he gives it to a king or a common soldier."

"Whereas," my husband told him, "I know that a man who keeps a king waiting while he forges a common soldier's sword is a man who in the king's sword will be forging the means to his own death."

"From olive harvest to the planting of the grain I have waited. Four long months in their season, and once each month I have traveled at your behest to claim that which I am rightfully owed. From olive harvest to the planting of the grain, you have each time turned me away with an excuse, so that I must believe you will never have time for my sword, though you had time enough to take my silver. Will you, then repay the sixty shekels of silver I have paid you for the sword you promised?"

"I have not had a moment to myself," I heard my husband lie. "I work from sunup to sundown, in backbreaking labor, and though I would not expect you to know it, the forging of an iron sword is an art near enough to magic that there can be little difference. The metal must be heated and hammered and folded and hammered and heated and hammered again, day after day, with each day's work bringing the metal closer to true. And I have the knowing of the art; on the fingers of one hand could I give you the men who know it near as well as I, and on no fingers at all could I give you the men who know it better! You wanted a sword made by a master? Well, you'll get one, but by all the gods and Baal first, you'll get it in your turn, and not before."

To which the young man sighed and turned away.

My husband might have worked from sunup to sundown some days. He was a busy man. But I knew as well as I knew my own name that he was making a number of bronze swords right then. He was making them for men from the army of Jabin, and for friends of Jabin's general Sisera—but he was not at that moment making any iron swords, for Jabin or anyone else.

I turned to look at Pigat, who had come to stand

beside me, as interested in what transpired on the other side of the tent as I was.

"Why did he say those things?" I whispered.

"You mean why did he lie?" Pigat laughed softly. "Because it suited him. The man is an Israelite. The Kenites have maintained their neutrality in this long war between Canaanites and Israelites because it's good for business to sell their smithing to both sides. But in the end, the Canaanites hold the fertile lowlands, and have the chariots and armies and wealth to keep the upstart Israelites confined to their poor highlands. So if Heber can take the man's silver, then keep him dangling like a hooked fish for his own amusement, he will. You'll hear him laughing about this tonight with his friends. They all do the same thing to some extent; they'll work for any who will pay them, because all silver spends the same. But they know, too, which goat gives the most milk."

"That's not right," I said.

"No. Of course not." Pigat shrugged. "But who are we to question those things our husband does? We are not smiths. We do not fashion metal, nor deal daily with men of high rank. Women have no place in the dealings of men."

I looked at her with curiosity. Pigat had, in one week, demonstrated to me that she held opinions on every subject under the sun, and that far from being the quiet and submissive woman I had thought her at our first meeting, she used every means at her disposal—flattery and wile and wit and guile and outright manipulation—to influence Heber when she thought the issue was one that mattered.

I had watched her with some admiration; she was not a woman who accepted "No" as an answer, just as a starting point. And most times she didn't even ask the question. "It's simpler," she told me early on, "if he thinks what he does is his own idea, whether it is to trade for more wool for the weaving, or to have new sandals made for all of us, or to lay in more wheat." She smiled a little. "He's very proud that he provides for us in such style—that he has more than one woman in his tent and still we are the first women in the camp with anything that is new or good."

The trick was, she said, to never let Heber find out that we were the ones bending him to our wills.

My husband's dishonesty with this soldier whose money he had taken was, I thought, something that mattered. I could not say for certain why it mattered to *me*.

If I closed my eyes, I could hear my father saying, "Not the promises he makes, but the promises he keeps, are the measure of the man."

Then, my mother would look at my sisters and me and say, "Honor is a luxury of men; women cannot afford it."

Were my husband found to be dishonorable in his dealings though, my sister-wives and I would suffer just as surely as he did. If men no longer bought from him, would we not share in his poverty? If he had no tent in which to sleep, would not the sky be our roof and the stones our beds as well?

Honor might be a luxury of men, but lack of honor could be the punishment of women all the same.

Neither Pigat nor Talliya thought the matter of any importance to them. But I did. And does not the one who sees the rat in the grain kill it?

This was my rat, though I did not know how I might hope to kill the beast.

I lifted up the jar I had let slide to the floor while I listened to Heber, and went out into the morning air, lost in thought as I made my way through the maze of clustered tents to the community well.

I reached the little square that surrounded the well. Tall, graceful terebinth and broad evergreen oaks shaded the square. One of the oaks held a shrine to Asherah. I bent a knee as I passed, but my sister-wives and I would need water to do the work of the day, and if I dallied any longer, I would make myself a stumbling block to all of us.

I sang:

> *"When the sorrows come,*
> *You can cry, cry, cry,*
> *Or take up your wings*
> *And fly, fly, fly."*

At the well, I put down the jugs on the damp earth. The other young wives had already come and gone.

Just as well, I thought. It would give me time to think.

"I would guess you more a doe than a calf," a deep voice said just behind me. "You sing like a sad little bird."

I jumped and turned, and found myself facing Levi of Kadesh, the handsome young soldier my husband was cheating.